Relics of War

ROMAN BERNARD

This book is dedicated to my wife

Cover illustration by
Erwin J. Arroza
ej.arroza@gmail.com

CHAPTER 1

Danny Ackerman Junior had only planned on smoking half a joint, but before he knew it, the joint was burned all the way down and his dad was on his way toward the car.

The windows were already open so the only thing Danny could do was pop a mint into his mouth and spray some air freshener that he always kept in the glove compartment.

He was still upset about having to wake up so early and he hoped his dad didn't give him a hard time about the weed, which he usually did.

Although Danny was a grown man of twenty-eight, his dad, Daniel Ackerman Senior, a lifelong military man, still intimidated him. It didn't matter that he was now almost seventy, losing his hair, wore thick glasses, and walked with a slight hunch, he would always be Major Ackerman.

His dad was wearing a pair of slip-on shoes, beige pants with an elastic waistband, and a cheap plastic windbreaker.

There was a substantial age gap between them because Danny's dad didn't get married until he was thirty-four-years-old. And although Danny's mother was twenty-four when they married, they didn't have children until after they were permanently stationed in the USA, which was almost seven years later.

Danny's dad swept a few napkins off the seat and struggled to climb into Danny's ten-year-old burgundy Hyundai SUV. "It's bad enough the DMV takes my license, now I have to smell this shit." His eyesight had faded quickly due to his worsening diabetes and he couldn't pass the vision test at his last license renewal.

"You know I have a prescription for medical marijuana." Replied Danny.

"Maybe if you didn't smoke so much of that . . . *medicine* . . . you would have the energy to clean up your car." He took a couple of candy wrappers and empty soda bottles from where his feet were and threw them behind the seat. "This is ridiculous."

Danny pulled away from the curb while wishing he had the money to buy his dad a smartphone and open a Lyft account for him. Or maybe there was a simpler, cheaper solution, like earplugs.

It was a bright sunny afternoon in southern California. Traffic was light so the ride to the hospital took only about ten minutes on the tree-lined freeway.

Danny was happy his dad didn't say anything when he opened a bottle of soda and took a slug. He had inherited his dad's sweet tooth, yet he knew he would never get diabetes like him because he had a secret weapon—weed. Or so he hoped.

After finding a parking spot as close to the main hospital building as possible so his dad wouldn't have to walk too far, Danny stepped out of his SUV and a bald-headed Asian monk wearing a red robe with an orange sash was right in front of him. Danny stepped back, hoping the man wasn't naked under that outfit.

The monk spoke with a heavy accent that Danny didn't recognize, "No man shall know the mind of Krishna."

"I don't have any money. Sorry." Danny maneuvered around the monk and toward his dad who was just closing the car door.

"Who's that guy?"

"One of those Hare Krishna's." Replied Danny. "Probably looking for money. He's barking up the wrong tree here."

"Watch out. You may start dressing like him if you take too much of that . . . *medicine*."

Both of them laughed while approaching the hospital entrance where a pair of sliding electric doors opened.

They were there to visit Danny's ninety-six-year-old grandfather who was recovering from a near-death bout of pneumonia.

Grandpa Ackerman was a small white-haired man, but

he was the toughest man Danny had ever known. The only man tougher than his dad.

This was the first time Danny had ever seen him seriously sick and hated seeing him in a hospital gown with a tube connected to his vein.

Inside Grandpa's room on the second floor, a nurse was checking his vitals. Danny and his dad stayed out of her way until she was finished, then they approached the bed.

Grandpa said, "That one there has the hots for me."

Danny chuckled while his dad shook his head.

"Bring those chairs closer and sit down." Grandpa glanced out into the hallway as if he was waiting for someone. "I have something important to tell you."

They sat down next to him and leaned in to hear his weakening voice.

Grandpa whispered, "I have a secret I've been hiding all these years."

Danny thought Grandpa was going to reveal a secret wife and children or something like that, but instead, the old man quickly handed Danny's dad a square wooden box almost the size of a PlayStation gamepad. The box had an eagle carved into the cover and ancient Germanic runes carved into the sides.

"Put it away." Demanded Grandpa.

Danny wanted to get a glance of what was in it, but his dad already had it in his jacket pocket.

Grandpa began talking about the war.

All his life, Danny had heard stories of his grandfather's conquests in North Africa and Italy during World War Two, however, he never spoke of his time fighting in Germany. He always said those missions were classified and he'd have to take that knowledge with him to his grave. But now he was ready to talk, and Danny was ready to listen.

Danny's dad was silent.

Grandpa began, "As you know, I was stationed in Italy as part of a special operations squad. The part I never told you boys is that after D-Day and the liberation of Paris, I was given my own squad. We were stationed at a temporary base in Northern Italy. I don't remember the exact day. I know it was October . . . October 1944. Yes . . . Hitler was on the run. Ike said the war would be over by Christmas. We all know how that turned out." He chuckled. "Did they expect us just to stroll into Berlin? Then there was the Ardennes . . . thank god I wasn't there for that mess."

It was either the weed, or the love for his grandfather, or a combination of both that made Grandpa's ramblings about the war interesting to Danny.

Danny's dad, however, never spoke about the Vietnam War despite the fact that he had served four tours there. He had always said he wanted Danny to join the military, but he had also always said he was happy for modern technology and that no one should have to fight another war like Vietnam again.

"You're getting off track, Pop." Danny's dad asked, "What's in the box?"

"The box. Yes. Feels like yesterday. It was an airborne mission . . . a night drop . . . right on the border of Germany and Austria. A secret Nazi weapons research facility that housed technology so advanced it was supposed to make their V2 rockets seem like bows and arrows. And those V2's were a real bitch. There was no way we were going to let the Russians get their hands on that type of technology." Grandpa glanced out into the hall again before lowering his voice and continuing his story. "Anyway . . . we were waiting for another squad deployed on land to disable the anti-aircraft guns in the forest before we could get our planes in the air. We finally got the okay and suited up."

Danny imagined as Grandpa told his story:

When Grandpa Ackerman was twenty-one-years-old, he had the same short thin body type he had as an old man. But unlike now, he was fast and nimble back then. His hair was blond rather than white and he still had the face of a baby. And despite his small physical stature, he was a natural born leader.

Flying into the darkness with only a bit of light from the half-moon above to guide them, ten soldiers dressed in black, perched in the belly of a Douglas C-47 Skytrain, which was basically a flying bus with propellers.

Grandpa Ackerman was known as Sergeant Ackerman back then, and like many other young men in that war, he had seen enough fighting and bloodshed to last a lifetime.

He was nervous, as he'd been in every combat situation, but he never showed it. Especially now that others were looking up to him.

Young Sergeant Ackerman pointed at a clearing in the forest ahead, then he gave the order to jump out of the huge propeller-driven plane and into the cold dark night.

Jumping was sometimes the worst part of the mission. They could be blown off course or land on something that could kill them. Not to mention, they were helpless slow-moving targets for anyone on the ground with a gun.

The icy air cut through Sergeant Ackerman's uniform and into his bones as he jumped out of the plane and plummeted toward the Earth, his organs pushing up inside of him—then, his parachute opened, which jerked him upward before reversing direction and finally drifting slowly downward. The tops of the trees nearby were barely visible as he got closer and hoped to land in the open area.

Sergeant Ackerman tucked and rolled when he landed, just as he'd been trained to do.

Luckily, no one had gone too far off course. They couldn't risk the Germans seeing a flare or even a flashlight.

Checking his compass and his map, the sergeant led his men through the forest until reaching a dirt road. The dirt road led down the mountain to a paved street, which they then followed to a lumber mill that was closed for the night.

Behind the building, the Americans met with two Austrian resistance fighters between huge stacks of logs.

Sergeant Ackerman couldn't help worrying about how quickly the entire squad could be wiped out if one of those log stacks fell down upon them.

The resistance fighters, two young men in tattered clothing, loaded the Americans onto a truck full of stacks of plywood. The sheets in the middle of the truck were set up to form an empty box that would house the soldiers. The two Austrians closed the box with a sheet of plywood on top and nailed it in place with only four nails, one in each corner.

In the dark box, the soldiers tried to keep from falling over each other as the truck took off down the dirt road and then began to pick up speed. They knew they were on the paved road when the ride became much smoother.

After about fifteen minutes, the truck slowed down and made a left turn. It slowed down even more after the turn, almost stopping.

Sergeant Ackerman whispered, "Time to go."

His squad forced the nailed sheet of plywood off the top of the box and climbed out.

The truck was rolling slowly as they climbed across stacks of plywood and then jumped off, landing in the brush at the side of the road.

There were houses down the road in a small town. Some of them still had their lights on.

Sergeant Ackerman gave the signal to move forward.

By the time the American soldiers crept through the trees toward the town, the truck was gone.

The resistance fighters explained that two years earlier, the Germans relocated everyone who had lived in the town and the houses were taken over by high ranking Nazis.

Sergeant Ackerman was relieved to know there was no chance of accidentally killing innocent civilians.

The road that entered the town was guarded by two Nazi soldiers who were easy to spot because of their burning cigarettes. Sergeant Ackerman wondered if there were any other guards hiding in the darkness. He told two men to watch their backs while the others moved forward.

The two stealthiest Americans, one a prize fighter from

Brooklyn, and the other a high school track star from Arizona, crept toward the guards and quickly slashed their throats. They kept their hands on the guards' mouths while slowly helping to guide their limp bodies on their way down to the ground, trying to avoid making any unnecessary noise.

Sergeant Ackerman made sure their cigarettes were extinguished. A forest fire would certainly alert their enemies of their presence. There may not have been a risk of fire due to the moisture of all the greenery around, but he wasn't taking any chances. Being thorough had saved his life on past missions.

Unsure of how many Germans were in the town, the Americans were on high alert.

Sergeant Ackerman led them quietly past the houses and toward the church.

The school, which was connected to the church, had allegedly been converted into the weapons research facility.

If they were unable to acquire the research, their orders were to destroy the facility at any cost, even if they had to give up their own lives to do so.

Two Nazi guards stood at attention, guarding the front entrance to the school.

Just as before, the same two stealthy Americans crept up slowly and simultaneously slashed the guards' throats, again helping the bodies drop quietly.

Sergeant Ackerman took the key ring from one of the corpses and stood to the side of the old wooden door while trying one of the keys. It didn't work, so he tried another, then another.

Finally, he found the right key and the door opened.

A guard stood there with a shotgun in his hand, he said something in German, then looked surprised when he saw the Americans dressed in black with their faces also blackened.

Sergeant Ackerman took advantage of the small window of opportunity when the Nazi hesitated. He already had his hand ready to draw his M1911 pistol from his shoulder holster. He'd been practicing with the extra weight of the bulky silencer so he would be ready for a situation just like this one. The sergeant whipped it out and fired a single shot into the Nazi's head. The body dropped.

The sergeant and his squad moved away from the door just in time. A Nazi inside the school fired a shotgun. That was the end of their operation being a covert one.

They entered the building with guns blazing.

Sergeant Ackerman locked and bolted the massive old door behind them and hoped that due to the sensitive technology in the school, they wouldn't use any heavy artillery to get through it.

The only windows were tiny stained glass panels within thick metal framing. Even if blown out, no human could fit through them.

The Americans all had flashlights attached to their Tommy guns. No point in using their pistols anymore.

Down the dark, silent hallway they crept.

Someone began knocking on the front door of the school while speaking German.

The Americans kept moving, down the hall, checking every nook and cranny for lurking enemies. There were doors on both sides, all of them locked.

The knocking at the front door turned into pounding and the speaking turned to yelling.

The Americans kept moving forward to the end of the hall. They turned the corner then stopped in front of a gigantic steel door that was obviously not from the original construction.

Sergeant Ackerman wondered why there weren't more guards. Maybe the intelligence was fake and there was nothing there. Or maybe it was a trap and they'd soon meet their deaths. No matter. They were already there, and they had a job to do. They knew the risks going in.

The sergeant gave the signal. The Americans slipped on their respirators and goggles, stepped back around the corner, and watched their rear while their demolition expert placed some newly developed C3 plastic explosives on the door hinges and the lock. He then inserted detonators and unrolled the wires until he was around the corner with the others, kneeling next to the sergeant.

While the Nazis were still pounding on the front door, they weren't trying to break through. That fact made Sergeant Ackerman feel slightly better. It meant there was definitely something sensitive in that building, but it also made him worry that the C3 they were about to blow could destroy whatever was behind that door.

Too late for second guessing. The sergeant crossed his fingers, then tapped his demolition man on the shoulder who then pressed the button that detonated the explosives.

They felt the blast vibrate the entire building as it cracked the old plaster walls in the hallway. The sound of the heavy steel door falling onto the marble floor echoed off the walls and ceilings, leaving a ringing in their ears.

When they turned the corner, the thick steel door was on the floor in one piece and smoke filled the doorway. They kept their masks on to avoid inhaling the toxic fumes.

With the only light coming from their flashlights, their field of vision was limited. They could only see in the direction they were pointing their guns.

Long tables filled most of the room. It was obviously the chow hall.

Sergeant Ackerman heard something behind him. He turned around. One of his men was on the ground. Dead. Neck broken. A rich boy from Connecticut who had proven his courage on many occasions in North Africa and Italy. Hand-picked by the sergeant for this team.

The sergeant didn't have time to feel guilty about the family who would never see that boy again. There would be plenty of time for guilt later.

He scanned the room and spotted something. An SS soldier creeping toward the track star from Arizona. The sergeant didn't want to use the Tommy gun since it was too hard to control, so he used his body to push his fellow American out of the way, then he reached for his pistol and shot the SS man three times, killing him instantly.

Another door opened to reveal another SS soldier who fired a shotgun, blasting the two Americans closest to the door, both of whom had just transferred to the unit after surviving D-Day in Normandy, both leaving behind young wives, one of them with two children.

The remaining Americans opened fire and killed two other Nazis who were trying to sneak into the room from the adjoining kitchen.

Obviously unused for quite some time, the dusty kitchen was now streaked with blood as well as flesh and bone fragments. Still, no secret research.

When they were sure there was no one else in the room with them, they crept down the stairs to the basement storeroom. Once again, the demolition man planted his charges, then they all hurried back up to the top of the stairs and waited in the kitchen for the explosion.

Sergeant Ackerman wondered what was going on outside. He hoped there was no other way into the building. And although he was willing to give up his life for his country, he was hoping he wouldn't have to.

After the explosion in the basement, they made their way back down the stairs, this time with only their bayonets in their hands. Their Tommy guns were strapped to their backs and their pistols holstered. They didn't know what type of equipment was in there, and they couldn't risk destroying it. The sergeant knew their good luck couldn't last forever.

Once inside the old basement storeroom, a tall massive SS man grabbed the first American in, a small black man from Detroit who knew more about cars than Henry Ford. He was a tough little guy, but he was no match against the SS man who twisted his arm, breaking it like a twig, and then took away his bayonet. The little man shrieked, but before the others were close enough to do anything, the SS man had buried the bayonet into the American's eye socket, deep enough to penetrate his brain, causing his body to flail around as it fell to the ground.

The other Americans slashed and stabbed at the hulking SS man with their bayonets, but he kept moving forward, taking their slices and stabs. Blood was everywhere, but he didn't stop. He grabbed one of them and strangled him while the others continued stabbing him. Blood was dripping from slashes and gouges on every part of his body, but he didn't release his grip, even after the young man's face was blue.

With his silenced pistol, Sergeant Ackerman fired a single shot into the SS man's temple. He dropped dead and so did the American he was strangling.

One American turned on the lights.

They were standing in a laboratory. Against one wall, beakers, test tubes, and burners occupied a workbench. On the opposite side was a thin lead dividing wall, and behind that, electronic components and circuit boards on another workbench. A metal file cabinet sat between two desks with stacks of folders and notebooks on them.

Sergeant Ackerman commanded, "Get those folders and notebooks first, then check the file cabinets."

A young soldier announced, "There's a door behind this bookshelf."

"Good eye." The sergeant and two others helped him move the tall, heavy bookshelf out of the way.

The door had an old-fashioned latch, but no lock. On the other side of the door was a long dark tunnel. The Sergeant pointed his flashlight into the musty darkness. "I hope this is our way out."

Another soldier yelled, "I found a safe."

Sergeant Ackerman turned to a young safe cracker from Chicago who had been arrested on his first offense and accepted the judge's offer to join the army rather than go to jail. The sergeant asked, "Can you open it?"

"Of course I can open it."

"Do it." The sergeant made sure all the research was

collected, then he turned back to the man working the safe with a stethoscope. They already had all the notebooks and folders, but he had to know what was in that safe, so he waited, impatiently, while glancing over his shoulder at their only way out.

Finally, when the safe was open, the only thing in it that seemed like it would be of importance to the military was four round metal film cases. The sergeant told them not to open the cases as the film could be delicate.

The safe also contained currency from many different countries and a few gold bars as well as a key in a small envelope for a safe deposit box. The envelope had French writing and an account number. Sergeant Ackerman pocketed the key and told his men to scoop up the cash and the gold.

He hated having to leave the bodies of his men, but that was his orders, as it often was on those types of missions. None of them had dog tags or any other way of identifying them.

The surviving Americans crept through the long dark tunnel until finally arriving at a metal ladder attached to the wall that led to a rusted manhole cover above.

The lowest ranked soldier climbed the ladder first and then released the latch and pushed the metal cover up.

Once he was partially outside, the sound of rapid, heavy-caliber machine gun fire erupted. The soldier's bloody body fell back down, without a head.

Sergeant Ackerman pulled the pin from a grenade, climbed part way up the ladder, and then lobbed the grenade outside. When it exploded, he heard men shrieking and yelling in German. He threw another one, waited for the explosion, then climbed out of the hole and opened up with his Tommy gun, not even knowing if there was anyone still there to shoot.

One by one, the remaining three American soldiers made their way to the surface and gunned down the wounded Nazis that were surrounding them.

Finally, the area was clear.

The sound of barking dogs and yelling Germans seemed far away, however, the sergeant knew they could still catch up with them.

He checked his compass and led what was left of his squad west through the cold forest for over three hours.

They were exhausted by the time they crossed the border into Switzerland.

Danny was jolted back to reality when a nurse entered the hospital room and Grandpa stopped talking.

She checked the monitors and wrote something in Grandpa's chart, then, before leaving the room, the nurse said, "Sorry guys . . . five more minutes. You'll have to come back this afternoon."

Danny wanted to know what was in that box in his dad's pocket. "What happened after you got to Switzerland, Grandpa?"

"We turned in all the research and the film cases to a Brit and an American who were waiting for us there. But we split up the cash and the gold."

Danny's dad shook his head. "Unbelievable."

"Don't judge me, son. We did it for the families of those who didn't make it back alive. You know those widows didn't get shit back then. They don't get shit now. We only took a small piece each so no one would have to worry about the others talking. We were all guilty. But most of it went to the widows . . . that's the god's honest truth."

Danny could tell that Grandpa's mind was drifting to other thoughts, so he asked, "What was in the research? And what about the Swiss deposit box key?"

Grandpa replied, "We never knew what was in that research. After we turned it in, they gave us train tickets and money and told us to go back to our temporary base in Northern Italy. They told us that we were to take that secret with us to our graves."

Daniel, Sr. replied, "Well . . . you just disobeyed that

order."

"Close enough. I'll be in my grave any minute now."

"Don't say that, Grandpa. The doctor said you'll probably be home in a couple of days."

Grandpa asked, "You want to know what happened with that key?"

Danny moved closer to hear his grandfather as he lowered his voice. Danny's dad shook his head in disapproval, yet he still leaned in to listen to what the old man had to say.

"After the war ended, most of us were stationed in Germany. I took a train to Switzerland while on leave. I thought I'd find more gold in that safe deposit box, instead, I found something else. That little wooden box."

Danny asked, "What's in it?"

Daniel, Sr. insisted, "Whatever it is, you should have turned it in."

Grandpa continued, "I was going to turn it in, but when I came out of the bank, two men tried to mug me . . . people don't get mugged in Switzerland. I fought them off long enough for a local cop to come and scare them away. I didn't make a report."

"But all these years . . . why didn't you give it to your commanding officer?"

Danny wanted to know what the hell was in the box while his dad only cared about why the old man hadn't followed protocol seventy years ago. Danny asked again, "What's in it?"

"Whatever it is . . . it's in my possession now. And I'm going to turn it in." Said Daniel, Sr.

Grandpa explained, "When I came back to the states, I had a visit from a Tibetan monk. He said that no government should have what is in that box. He said that it couldn't be destroyed, so it must be hidden forever. I acted like I didn't know what he was talking about, and I didn't have it with me. But, he knew I was lying. It was in my safe deposit box at the bank all this time. When I first felt sick last week . . . well . . . I guess I just knew my time was up. How long can I live . . . right? So I took it out of the bank and kept it with me."

Danny would have wondered if his grandfather was just high from whatever they were giving him and had imagined the whole story, but then he had to worry about his own sanity if hallucinating monks was a family trait. He knew there was no weed in the world that could have made him hallucinate the monk in the parking lot. "A monk said some Hare Krishna stuff to me before . . . out there in the parking lot . . . just before we came in."

"They've been watching me since the war."

Daniel, Sr. asked, "Do you actually believe that Tibetan monks have been watching you for the past seventy-three years?"

"Don't talk to me like that, son. I may be old, but I still have all my marbles."

Daniel, Sr. asked, "Okay. What is it? And how did you get it back to America? Wait . . . I don't want to know how you got it here. Just tell me what it is. Am I going to go to prison for having it?"

Grandpa glanced out the door at the nurse who was on her way there. "Looks like they're coming to give me my sponge bath. My favorite part of the day." He winked at Danny, then turned to Danny's dad and whispered, "Just hide that thing. We'll talk more about it later. Don't make any decisions yet."

When the nurse entered, Danny and his father stepped out of the room.

All the way home, Danny pestered his dad. He wanted to know what was in the box, but his dad refused to open it. He said, "He's just high from the morphine."

"Then why won't you open it?"

"Just in case there's something in there that's dangerous or contagious . . . or just disgusting. Don't worry, if it turns out to be nothing, then you can have the box. You can use it to keep your . . . *medicine* . . . in."

Danny wouldn't admit it, but that exact thought had already crossed his mind.

Finally, he pulled into his dad's driveway and dropped him off. He waited for him to open the door to his one-story ranch house and go inside, then, Danny lit up the clip from the joint he'd smoked earlier and pulled out of the driveway, cranking up some classic rock as he cruised down the block.

CHAPTER 2

Alex Pavlov, a Russian operative whose official title was diplomatic attaché to the Russian ambassador in Los Angeles, had just received new, classified, high-priority orders.

A Russian mole in the CIA had just proven his worth once again by giving them invaluable information.

Alex and two other Russian men in suits sat in traffic in a new black Mercedes E-class on the 405 freeway for at least an hour before arriving at their destination: Sunnydale, a quiet suburban city in Orange County.

They changed freeways and cruised for the next fifteen minutes with no traffic to a quiet neighborhood that consisted of one-story ranch houses that had been built in the sixties, each with a different color siding. Most of the houses had palm trees out front and orange trees in the back. Here and there, the original houses had been replaced by newer, larger houses, especially on the more spacious corner lots.

Just before arriving at their destination, Alex' phone vibrated. There was a text message on an internet app from an unregistered number that showed a picture of the man he was to question, a retired army major named Daniel Ackerman. Unless the man was a survivalist nut or a psycho conspiracy theorist, Alex wasn't expecting any resistance as the major was almost seventy years old and suffered from diabetes.

After deleting the message from his phone, Alex parked his Mercedes across the street and a few houses down from where he was going, then he spoke in Russian when he told the other two men to wait for him in the car.

Out of the corner of his eye, for just a moment while crossing the street, he thought he saw someone in red. When he turned to get a better look, no one was there.

He then strolled along the sidewalk to Daniel, Sr.'s house. When he knocked on the door, a balding white man with thick glasses answered. The same man he'd just seen in the picture on his phone. He knew it was him, but he still had to ask. Alex tried to hide his Russian accent when he spoke, "Daniel Ackerman?"

"Who are you?"

"I am an attorney. I am handling your father's estate. May I come in?"

"My father doesn't have an estate. Who hired you?"

The old man's mind was obviously still sharp. Alex knew he wouldn't be able to bullshit his way in, and he didn't have time to waste, so he did it the old fashioned way. He whipped out his Glock and forced his way into the immaculate house. "Who else is here?"

Daniel, Sr. replied, "Major Daniel Ackerman. Serial number . . ." He then began to recite his serial number.

Alex slapped him. "You fucking Americans. I should kill you right now."

"Then do it."

"Don't tempt me." Alex surveyed the room, then demanded, "Tell me where it is."

"There's no money or drugs here if that's what you're after."

"What? Do you see this suit? This suit costs more than your fucking furniture. I'm not here for money. Where is the box your father gave you?"

"Major Daniel Ackerman. Serial number . . ." He began to recite his serial number again, but this time his face was met with Alex' fist. He stumbled backward, almost falling down, but he refused to give in. Once again, he recited, "Major Daniel Ackerman. Serial number . . ."

Alex hit him so hard that he dropped instantly.

CHAPTER 3

After dropping off his dad, Danny had spent only ten minutes on the freeway getting home.

When he entered the quiet mobile home park where he lived, he turned off the classic rock that he'd been blaring from his radio and slowed down to a crawl. He passed palm trees and shrubs while gently rolling over speed bumps.

A few inquisitive old people peeked out their front windows as he passed.

The mobile homes were basically metal boxes with windows, sitting on cinderblock foundations concealed by metal siding. And while they weren't exactly like real houses, they were spacious and comfortable, and some of them were actually beautiful with small manicured lawns and flower gardens. Not durable enough for states with hurricanes or tornadoes, but good enough for sunny southern California.

Danny turned the corner and passed the fenced-in swimming pool that was technically still open, but didn't have a lifeguard now that summer was over. He never used the pool anyway. His pudgy pale body burnt within a few minutes of being in the sun and all he could do in the water was doggy paddle.

He continued slowly past a few adjoining roads until reaching the back row where his beige and brown mobile home stood between a newer blue and white unit and a small building that housed the garbage dumpsters and maintenance worker's tools.

When Danny was about to graduate high school, he took and passed the ASVAB test with high scores. All his life he had wanted to join the army just like his father and grandfather before him, however, by the time he was sixteen and his mother was long gone, he'd changed his way of looking at the world and no longer wanted to live a military life. The night before his physical, he smoked as much weed as his lungs could hold so he would fail the drug test and have no chance of getting in.

After his father learned what he'd done, he threw Danny out of the house. That night, Danny was in a car with his friends when a truck lost control and smashed them. Danny suffered a broken arm and his lawyer threw in whiplash and lower back pain. They all sued and made good money. After the doctor's and lawyer's fees, Danny was left with enough money to buy his mobile home, which was cheaper than most due to its age and its location next to the garbage containers.

He still had to pay maintenance and utilities, but after the accident, and applying three times, he was finally awarded permanent social security disability, which was enough for him to get by, but didn't leave much extra.

Danny parked his SUV under the awning next to his unit, which only had a few feet of space between his driveway and the next unit, then he climbed the five stairs to his front door and unlocked it.

Inside, two black and white cats that were brother and sister and named Bruce and Selina, had free reign of the place, which was a mess of dirty clothes, empty soda bottles, and food wrappers. Even worse than his car.

He often found himself having to wash his underwear in the sink because he'd been too lazy to do a wash. The mobile home park had its own Laundromat for residents, and it was half the price of those open to the public, but his laziness and procrastination always got the best of him. One of the many reasons his ex-girlfriend had given when dumping him.

After filling the cats' bowl with fresh water, Danny searched for something that was putting off a putrid odor. He threw out a couple of old food containers and emptied the cat litter box, but the odor was still there. Eventually, he gave up his search for the source of the smell and lit an incense stick hoping that would make it disappear, at least temporarily.

From his bedroom, he retrieved a glass jar that he kept

his weed in and then thought about the little wooden box that his father had. Most people would have opened it, even if they were planning on turning it in, yet Danny knew he could count on his father not to open it. His father never broke the rules.

He plopped down onto the living room sofa and rolled a couple of joints on the coffee table. And then, before heading back outside, he took a slug of soda from a warm two-liter bottle he had forgotten to put in the refrigerator last night. And he still didn't put it in the refrigerator. He just headed out the front door.

Outside, an old woman with skin like leather from years of sun tanning, dozed off on a rocking chair in the doorway of a faded green mobile home across the street. She resembled a reptile absorbing the sun's rays.

On foot, Danny snuck along the back of the mobile homes on his side of the street, then, when he was sure the old woman couldn't see him, he crossed over to her side and snuck along the back of those mobile homes until arriving at the back of her unit. He tapped on the window.

An overweight man in his fifties with a thick gray beard and glasses peered out the filthy glass.

Danny whispered, "Skywolf, it's me, Danny."

Everyone called him Skywolf, and although people had asked him in the past, no one knew his real name. Skywolf opened the back door. Danny always hoped to hear his mother slip and say his real name, however, he wasn't there often enough to catch it.

Danny entered and followed Skywolf into his bedroom, which consisted of a similar mess to the one in his house, but instead of an unknown odor, the room reeked of cigarette smoke and ashes. One shelf was kept perfectly clean—Skywolf's action figure shelf. Mostly Star Wars figures and superheroes. Some of them still in the package and worth serious money to collectors. Danny spoke in a loud whisper, "Your mom is sitting by the front door."

Skywolf had only been to Danny's mobile home once.

He couldn't stop sneezing and scratching due to his extreme allergy to cats. So every time they hung out, they did so at Skywolf's place, even though his mother didn't allow him to have guests because one of his friends had stolen a crystal ashtray twenty years ago.

Skywolf said, "Don't worry. She'll be sleeping most of the time. You bring any weed?"

"Of course." Danny lit up one of the joints that he had just rolled, took a puff, and handed it to him.

Skywolf smoked while powering up his PC. "I got the source codes for the new Doom game."

"No one has those yet. How are you getting them?"

Skywolf took a deep hit and then spoke while holding his breath, "That kind of information could cost you your life."

"Fuck you."

They both laughed.

Skywolf coughed the entire time they smoked the joint, yet he still lit a cigarette after they finished, filling the room with even more smoke.

"Man. At least open a window."

"Open it." Skywolf sat down in front of his computer and began punching keys on the keyboard.

Danny opened the window and then turned back to see his new desktop, a picture of Skywolf's face comically superimposed over that of a male porn star in the shower with two hot women. "It's the same thing every time." Danny said, "You should do one with a midget."

Skywolf replied, "It's not the same. This is my first shower picture . . . well, my first shower picture with *two* girls. But I'll do one with a midget . . . I'd do a midget in real life, too. If she was hot." He turned his head and asked, "Did my mom just say something?"

"I didn't hear anything."

Skywolf opened his bedroom door, stuck his head out into the hallway, and yelled, "Did you say something, mom?"

She replied, "Someone is knocking on your friend's door!"

Danny stayed in the bedroom and stayed quiet while Skywolf went to talk to his mother.

After a few minutes, he returned and whispered, "A guy in a suit is at your place. I don't know, man. He looks like a cop to me."

Danny couldn't conceive why the cops would be after him, but he didn't have the balls to confront him, so he and his friend snuck out the back door and around the side where they tried to peek over a wooden fence and see what was going on.

They caught a glimpse of a man in a shiny gray suit standing in front of Danny's mobile home, then they ducked back down behind the fence.

Danny whispered, "That guy doesn't look like a cop to me." He tried to peek through a thin opening in the fence but was only able to see Skywolf's mother sitting in her chair. No matter how he changed his angle, he wasn't able to see the man.

Skywolf opened his mouth to say something, but then he stopped and listened.

The man had a Russian accent. "Excuse me."

Danny tried to slow his breathing and hear what was being said while still staring through the crack in the fence.

The man asked Skywolf's mother, "Do you know the boy who lives in that mobile home?"

She spoke with a raspy voice from decades of cigarette smoking. "Are you the police?"

"His name is Danny Ackerman. Do you know him?"

The old lady coughed a few times then took another cigarette from her pink leather case and lit it with a match. When she inhaled, the smoked seemed to have cured her cough. She said, "I'm sorry, but I have to see your badge. There's been a lot of burglaries around here lately. And a woman was raped just down the street."

There was another male voice that Danny recognized.

The mobile home park security guard. The security guard asked, "May I help you, sir?"

The man in the suit was obviously trying to downplay his Russian accent when he said, "I'm a lawyer. I was just trying to locate a client of mine."

Skywolf was about to light a cigarette. Danny stopped him, worried that they might hear it or follow the smell and find them hiding.

The security guard responded to the Russian man, "I can give him a message if you like."

"Thank you. But that won't be necessary. I'll be seeing him tomorrow anyway."

Danny was surprised to hear Skywolf's nosy mother ask, "What does that boy need with a lawyer?"

"I'm handling his grandfather's estate. Unfortunately, the old man may not be with us much longer."

Danny's grandfather had a car and a house that both needed major work. There was no estate to settle, and the old man had no money in the bank after spending most of his life savings a few years earlier trying to cure his dying wife. He had no lawyer.

CHAPTER 4

Alex Pavlov strolled away from the old woman's mobile home and toward the guest parking lot knowing that the security guard would be watching him until he was gone.

When he had checked out Danny's mobile home earlier, he noticed a gate blocking the back entrance, and he also noticed that the gate had a chain and a lock on it.

As he drove out of the mobile home park, he waved at the security guard who was now on his way toward a small building with a sign on the door that read: *Office*.

Alex knew Danny had been home recently. The hood of his car was still warm. Either he went somewhere on foot, or someone picked him up in a vehicle, or, he was still somewhere in the mobile home park, maybe even hiding silently in his home.

Alex parked in a shopping center parking lot across the street and then scrolled through the contacts on Daniel Ackerman's phone until arriving at Danny Ackerman Junior.

Alex sent Danny a text message.

CHAPTER 5

Danny wondered if the man looking for him could have been from the government. Maybe they were finally prosecuting hackers who stole source codes and cracked expensive computer games just so they could post them online for people to play for free.

Then he considered the man's accent and his marijuana-induced imagination made him wonder if the Russians were after him. Maybe the Kremlin wanted him to work as a political troll for them, or hack government secrets for them.

When he considered how expensive the man's suit looked, he entertained the possibility that he could be from the Russian mob and they wanted him to hack into credit card and bank accounts. He was sure he could make some serious money that way, but he was also sure that he could end up a headless corpse somewhere if he fucked up somehow, and he had a life long history of fucking up. He would have to refuse and hope they don't kill him just for saying no.

Of course, he realized he was letting his imagination get the best of him once again. But, no matter who the man in the suit was, Danny knew something wasn't right.

After he left, they had returned to Skywolf's room where Danny lit up another joint to soothe his nerves.

He almost hit the ceiling when his cell phone beeped.

Taking a deep breath, Danny checked his phone to find a text message from his dad. He was surprised because he knew that his dad hated texting.

The message read: *I have your father. I will kill him if you do not give me the relic. I know your grandfather gave it to you. One hour. The Sunnydale Mall. South entrance. If you are not there, I will kill him. If you contact the police, I will kill him.*

Danny had a feeling the message was from the Russian who was just looking for him.

Whatever was in that box was not worth his father's life.

He imagined his stubborn father refusing to give it up and he hoped whoever was after him didn't hurt him. He also wondered why they thought he had it. His father wouldn't have told them that.

CHAPTER 6

Alex had been sitting in his black Mercedes for forty minutes and hadn't gotten a response from Danny. He just hoped that Danny was on his way to the mall with the relic.

Danny's father was being held in the back of a van near the mall by another Russian operative.

After another five minutes, Alex decided to go. He only needed ten minutes to get to the mall, but he didn't want to be late, so he started the car and headed down the wide sunny street while checking his rearview mirror just in case Danny showed up at the last minute.

As he pulled into the spacious mall parking lot and parked near a row of short palm trees, he thought about how nice it would be to retire in California. He was proud to be Russian, and he was proud that his father and uncles were all KGB agents during the reign of the Soviet Union. However, he wasn't looking forward to going back to his claustrophobic apartment in cold gray Moscow.

The only problem with California was the palm trees. All his life he'd loved palm trees, which he had only seen in movies, but now, every time he saw palm trees, they reminded him of Israel, and when he thought of Israel, he remembered Ingrid. And not remembering Ingrid was the one thing he struggled with on a daily basis. No matter how much time passed, Alex could still smell her perfume and taste the red wine on her lips.

After parking his car, he cleared his head before strolling into the mall through the south entrance.

A group of middle-aged women flirted with him as he pretended to read the directory map, asking him if he needed any help. Alex thanked them and told them that he already found what he was looking for.

CHAPTER 7

Danny snuck along the back of the mobile homes and then scoped out the area before removing a lock that wasn't actually locked from the gate blocking the back entrance.

The garbage trucks came at all different times, and as both security guards were getting along in age, they were tired of locking and unlocking the gate, so they left the lock on the chain in a way that it appeared locked, but wasn't. Danny knew that because he'd often invited one of the guards over to smoke with him.

Fortunately, the rusted old noisy gate that had been there for many years had been replaced a year earlier and the new gate rolled smoothly on wheels in a metal track embedded into the asphalt.

Danny made sure no one was watching while he rolled the gate open and then cruised slowly out of the mobile home park and onto the street in his burgundy SUV.

That tiny bit of physical activity had him out of breath and his heart was racing. He felt guilty about leaving the gate open and hoped the security guard would notice it before the manager did, but a possible reprimand about an open gate couldn't make Danny abandon his father who was in mortal danger.

He had no idea what he would do, yet that didn't stop him from driving to his father's house.

When he arrived, he found the front door partially open. Danny pushed it open the rest of the way and noticed broken furniture and a mess everywhere. His father kept everything spotless. He wouldn't even leave a newspaper on the coffee table.

Danny called out, "Dad? Dad, you here?" The smell of his dad's favorite lunch, tomato soup and grilled cheese, was still lingering in the air.

Just then, a man who resembled a pitbull in a suit appeared from the kitchen and pointed a gun at Danny.

With an even thicker Russian accent than the man from

the mobile home park, he said, "You were supposed to go to the mall. Give me the relic and we will let your father go."

Danny was trembling. He was barely able to spit the words out, "I don't have it."

The man approached him, slipped his gun into his jacket, and punched Danny in the face.

Dizzy and confused, Danny stumbled, almost falling back. Blood dripped from his lip as a tear dripped from his eye. "I would give it to you if I had it. I swear. I don't even know what it is. I just want my dad to be okay."

The man grabbed Danny by the throat with both hands and squeezed.

Danny tried to pry the strong hands from his throat, but he was just too weak. He saw spots. Everything began to fade away. His hands dropped to his sides. He couldn't even beg for his life.

A woman's voice exclaimed, "Hands in the air!"

The man released his grip on Danny's neck.

Danny collapsed onto the floor and gasped for air like a fish that had just been pulled out of the water.

When he looked up, he saw a stunningly beautiful blonde woman with piercing blue eyes, wearing a black skirt suit, and pointing a gun at the Russian.

When Danny was finally able to get some oxygen into his lungs, he struggled to his feet while bracing himself on a broken end table. His breathing was still restricted as he put his hand on his bruised neck.

The Russian reached for his gun, but before he could shoot, the woman fired a shot into his skull.

The crack of the gunshot echoed off the walls.

Danny's brain buzzed.

The man's body fell to the floor, convulsing. Blood pouring out of the bullet hole in his head.

Danny froze. He'd never seen a person killed before in real life. It was so much different than in a video game.

The woman kicked the gun out of the man's reach and then fired a second shot into his head, splattering more blood and brains around before turning and pointing her gun at Danny who was trembling, his ears still ringing.

Barely above a whisper, Danny begged, "Don't shoot."

"I'm not going to shoot you. I'm here to help you." She lowered her gun and then pulled out a leather wallet and showed him her CIA credentials. "I am Agent Victoria Becker." She rummaged through the dead man's suit until finding a cell phone, which she then removed the battery from before slipping it into her jacket pocket. While checking the corpse's other pockets, she asked Danny, "Do you know what this man was looking for?"

It took a moment for Danny to catch his breath and get his thoughts together, then he stammered, "No . . . yes . . . um . . . I think so. Something in a little wooden box, but I don't know what it is. And I don't have it. My grandpa gave it to my dad . . . and my dad said he was going to turn it in. Then I got a message that they took my dad and they want the box . . . but I don't have it."

"If your father had it, the Russians wouldn't have taken him. And they wouldn't have left this guy here. We need to move fast. Tell me everything that happened after your grandfather gave your father the box."

"Nothing. I dropped off my dad, then I . . ." Danny was embarrassed to tell the gorgeous woman in front of him that he plays video games, so he left that part out when he told her, "I went to visit a friend. That's when a guy was at my house looking for me. Another Russian. Then I got this text from my dad's phone. My dad never texts."

Danny tried to slow his hand from trembling long enough for her to read the text message threatening his father's life.

Victoria asked, "Did your father have the box in his hand when he got out of your car?"

"No. It was still in his pocket . . . his jacket pocket."

"Did his jacket pocket have a zipper?"

"How am I supposed to know that?"

Danny could hear sirens in the distance.

Victoria led him out of the house. "Let's check your car. Maybe it fell out of his pocket."

When Danny opened the passenger side door, the little wooden box was there, on the filthy floor mat among the garbage. He picked it up and showed her, hoping to take her attention away from his messy car.

The sirens became louder. Obviously getting closer.

Victoria glanced over her shoulder and said, "Let's go. You drive." She nudged him into his car.

Danny felt it was suspicious that she wanted to get out of there before the cops arrived. Then he thought about all the movies he'd seen and how different agencies were always fighting over jurisdiction.

Of course, her ID could have been fake. She could have saved his life just long enough for him to find the box. He had no reason to trust her, other than her incredible beauty, but for a man who hadn't got laid in months, that was enough to make him get in his car and drive away, ignoring the cops speeding toward his father's house from the opposite way.

Victoria said, "I'll come back for my car later. We need to get to the university right away."

Danny replied, "University? Why?"

CHAPTER 8

Tsomo, the Tibetan monk who had approached Danny earlier in the hospital parking lot, had flown into LAX from China in the middle of the night. His red robe and leather sandals were obviously out of place, yet not many people paid attention to him as there were also Indian women wearing traditional robes as well as Muslim men and women who were covered from head to toe in non-western clothing. But, he still hoped that his contact would have American clothes waiting for him.

There were two people who had their eyes on him a bit too much at the airport. A white man and a black woman who were failing to blend in with the other airline passengers. Tsomo knew how strict airport security was in America, so that made it obvious that the couple who was following him had important friends.

He gawked at his surroundings with a fake look of confusion on his face while strolling down the wide hallway with just a carry-on sized leather bag around his shoulder.

When he noticed a crowd of people coming out of another gate, he slipped in between them, and when they passed the restroom, he pretended to enter the restroom, but then quickly slipped out of sight and hurried down the hall and outside, where he jumped into the first taxi he saw.

He watched out the back window to be sure he wasn't being followed as the morning sun became visible on the horizon.

Although Tsomo had been studying English for the past ten years, he still had trouble with it, as there were no fluent speakers in his mountaintop village in Tibet. Fortunately, like his out of place clothing, there were plenty of people in America whose English was much worse than his. Even the taxi driver who had taken him to his motel from the airport spoke less English than he did.

A motel room was already rented for him and the key was waiting at the front desk. Tsomo knew there was no time to sleep so he was thankful for the few hours he had slept on the plane from China. He hadn't eaten since the airport in Beijing and his stomach was growling, but he had to ignore it. He only had time for a quick shower, skipping his daily meditation.

After retrieving a car key from the top drawer of the night table, Tsomo went outside into the motel parking lot where a compact beige rental car was waiting for him.

Inside the car was an unregistered cell phone with a few apps already installed. The only number stored in the phone didn't have a name. It was a direct line to his contact in America.

The location of the relic could only be tracked from Tibet, then the information had to be called into China, where it was then relayed to Tsomo through an internet messenger app, so there was sometimes a delay in knowing the exact location of the relic.

There was a sheathed hunting knife and some American clothes in the trunk of the rental car, but as per his contact's advice, he had gone straight to the hospital and caught Major Daniel Ackerman and his son, Danny, just as they were parking and getting out of their car.

After they had entered the hospital, Tsomo bought two packs of crackers from the vending machine in the lobby, then scarfed them down while waiting in his car in the parking lot until the two men came back out.

He then followed them to the father's house and waited there as the son drove away, assuming, or more like hoping, that the son didn't have the relic.

Still waiting for a message from China, Tsomo stepped out of his compact beige rental car to retrieve the clothes from the trunk when he noticed three white men in suits approaching in a black Mercedes.

At first, he thought they were just driving by, but then, when they made a U-turn, Tsomo stepped to the side and watched.

When the driver had gotten out of the car, Tsomo was

sure he had spotted him. Fortunately, he was fast enough and thin enough to disappear behind a thick ancient sycamore tree.

Tsomo wasn't sure who they were, but he knew they were there for the relic when after a few minutes, the driver of the Mercedes came out of the house dragging Daniel Ackerman, Sr. who was unconscious. The other two men jumped out of the Mercedes and helped the driver carry their prisoner to the trunk of the car.

Armed only with the hunting knife, Tsomo decided not to fight against three men who were probably armed with guns. He knew they didn't have the relic anyway. If they had it, they wouldn't have needed to kidnap the father. Tsomo assumed the son had it if it wasn't still in the house. He knew it was no longer at the hospital.

Hiding down low in the driver's seat of his rental car and still waiting to hear news from China on the relic's current location, Tsomo decided to check the house just in case it was still in there, hidden somewhere.

When the Mercedes was about to drive away, the man who had been sitting in the back got out and entered the house.

Tsomo had a feeling he'd be wasting time sitting there. He texted his contact and asked about Danny. She already had the information ready to forward. As he read through Danny's bio, he was surprised that someone who grew up in a country with so many opportunities had made nothing of himself.

After about twenty minutes, just as Tsomo was considering leaving his post to search for Danny at his mobile home, Danny pulled up in his burgundy SUV, parked in his father's driveway, and then got out and approached the door.

Still dressed in nothing except his robe and sandals, Tsomo grabbed the hunting knife, and just as he was about to get out of the car, he noticed an attractive white woman in a black skirt suit sneaking into the house with a gun in her hand. He wondered who she was and how she had slipped past him.

When he stepped out of the car with the hunting knife in his hand, he heard gunshots inside the house. If the neighbors saw a monk in a red robe carrying a knife, they would certainly call the police, so Tsomo slipped back into his rental car and tried to stay hidden. Whoever left the house alive was the person he'd be following.

To his surprise, the two people who had come out of the house alive were the attractive woman and Danny.

They then searched Danny's SUV and obviously found something before driving away. He assumed it was the relic.

Tsomo surveyed the cars parked in the area and wondered which car the woman had been driving. He also considered the fact that someone could have dropped her off and was waiting for her somewhere.

He started up his rental car and followed Danny's SUV as a cop car with its sirens flashing sped up the block from the opposite way, toward the house.

While following Danny and the woman, Tsomo stayed so far back that he almost lost them a few times.

Compared to his quaint mountaintop home, the streets in California were so wide and everything was so spread out, Tsomo was worried that they would spot him following them. He kept checking his phone for a message from China while trying to remember all the American driving rules, and at the same time, trying not to lose sight of Danny's burgundy SUV.

CHAPTER 9

The Sunnydale Police Station was a one-story white concrete building with tinted windows and a parking lot next to it. A strip of thick green grass surrounded all four sides as well as a flower-lined walkway to the front entrance from the parking lot. The back entrance was reserved for those in custody.

Detective Trevor Robertson, a six-foot-tall, thirty-one-year-old former marine with short-cropped blond hair had just been promoted from narcotics to homicide after the old homicide detective had to retire due to his Parkinson's disease becoming too much to control. Detective Robertson doubted himself, despite the fact that his coworkers and his wife kept telling him he was capable.

Sunnydale was the smallest city in Orange County and its biggest problem was spoiled blue-collar children who grew up to be drug addicts still living at home. There was a bit of cocaine and heroin around, but most of the people in the area preferred prescription opioids—and then there were the methamphetamine users who could be spotted from a mile away. Marijuana had been legal in California long before Robertson joined the police force. He could only imagine how chaotic things must have been when they had to arrest people for weed as well.

The former junior homicide detective, who had just been promoted to senior homicide detective, was busy in court when the call came in to the homicide desk, so Robertson took the case.

A neighbor reported hearing gunshots and when a uniformed cop arrived, he found the house destroyed and an unidentified corpse with two bullet holes in the head.

Detective Robertson printed out a copy of the report and then drove his unmarked gray police car less than a mile to find a group of gawking neighbors gathered around the house. He told the uniformed cops to make the crowd disperse and then he entered the house.

Inside, it was obvious by the way the house had been torn apart that someone was searching for something. He knew that a retired army Major lived there, but no one knew where the Major was. Robertson wondered if the old man could have been surprised by a burglar and shot him and then fled out of fear. Then he considered the dead man's suit and the gun they found on the floor, and he didn't believe he was just a common burglar.

The only time Robertson had worn a suit in the past was to weddings and funerals, and it was the same black suit he'd used for years. He'd only recently been shopping for new suits since his promotion to homicide detective, and he didn't remember anything like the shiny material the dead man was wearing at the warehouse store where he and his wife had gone. He glanced down at his own navy blue suit and it reminded him of a kid going to Sunday school.

Maybe the dead man was a Hitman who had underestimated the old major. Or maybe he was looking for government secrets. Detective Robertson considered every possibility, no matter how ridiculous. If he couldn't show any progress on the case, he knew the county sheriff's office or even the state police could take over, and he didn't want that. Not on his first case.

He took pictures and measurements and took notes until the county forensics team arrived.

When he went back outside, he noticed that the door had not been forced or damaged. He couldn't even see any evidence that the lock had been picked.

With his notepad in his hand, he spoke with the few neighbors who were outside of their houses watching.

An old couple who lived across the street had been sitting in their front room with a perfect view of the house when they heard the gunshots. They told the detective that Danny, Jr. came out of the house with a woman in black just after the shots were fired. The son and the woman then sped away in Danny's burgundy SUV.

While questioning the other neighbors door to door,

Robertson heard different versions of the story. Some people heard two shots while others heard only one. A home attendant at the end of the block mentioned seeing a bald Asian man in a red robe and sandals hiding behind a tree.

With no useful information, Robertson returned to the thrashed house where the forensics team was still going through the mess and dusting for fingerprints.

He looked around once more to be sure he didn't miss any important details, then he gave the okay for two people from the county coroner's office to take the body to the morgue.

They lifted the corpse onto a stretcher and covered it with a white sheet before rolling it outside and into their van that was parked half on the front lawn.

CHAPTER 10

Still at the mall waiting for Danny to arrive, Alex Pavlov strolled along the polished beige marble walkway while gazing into brightly lit store windows admiring expensive clothes and shoes on mannequins. A security guard walked by once but didn't even glance at him.

More than ten minutes had passed since the time Danny was supposed to have been there. Alex waited another five minutes then called the man he had left at Danny's dad's house. No answer. The voicemail had never been set up because they were all using unregistered phones.

After another five minutes, Alex tried the phone again, and again, but there was no answer.

He drove back to the quiet neighborhood and followed the maze of identical streets to the house where he found two cop cars with their sirens flashing.

When Alex saw the white coroner's van driving away, he knew his man was in there. He then wondered who had gotten to him and if that person had the relic. It obviously wasn't the kid who had spent most of his life watching television and playing video games who had killed a well-trained Russian operative.

He still wasn't sure that Danny had the relic, but he decided to text him again anyway. Alex replaced the battery into Danny's dad's phone and typed: *I told you to meet me at the mall. Now I will break one of your father's arms as punishment. You have two hours to bring the relic to the mission at San Juan Capistrano. Come alone. This is your last chance. I will kill your father if I do not get it.*

CHAPTER 11

After parking his SUV in a three-story brick parking structure across the street from the university, Danny rummaged through his seat divider searching for a snack, but the only thing edible he found was a bag of marijuana gummy candies. He popped a half of a gummy into his mouth as Victoria stepped out of the car.

Danny slipped the package into his pocket. Of course, the candies did nothing for his hunger, but his high was fading and he didn't have anything to smoke. He wouldn't have smoked in front of Victoria anyway.

After walking down the concrete stairs and then leaving the parking structure, Danny and Victoria strolled across an eight-lane street with a palm tree divider running down the center. A cool breeze made the bright sun overhead feel welcome.

Danny was a couple of inches shorter than Victoria and his faded sweatshirt, ripped jeans, and old sneakers didn't match her conservative yet elegant attire, but that didn't stop him from holding his head high while college students passed them in the crosswalk. He wanted to reach down and hold her hand, but he knew she could easily break his arm, so he didn't attempt it.

He noticed a Starbuck's and asked Victoria, "You thirsty?"

"Later. We don't have much time."

His high was fading fast and he was craving something sweet to munch on. He wasn't used to all this excitement and running around. He usually took a nice nap in the afternoon after having his snack. His energy levels were low, but he didn't want Victoria to know it.

The university was a red brick building with limestone trim that featured arches and a turret. It looked more like a castle than a college.

They entered the lobby, and before they approached the front desk, two men greeted them.

One man was statuesque with black and gray hair and pale gray eyes that reminded Danny of a wolf. Wearing a matte black suit and tie, he spoke with a slight Texan accent. "You must be Danny. Hello. I am Professor Wilhelm Wagner."

The other man had glasses and a beard and wore a brown sweater over his shirt and tie. "Dave Black. Nice to meet you." He spoke to both Danny and Victoria at the same time, however, his eyes were only on Victoria.

Danny recognized Dave Black. "I know you. Well . . . I don't know you . . . but I've seen you . . . on TV."

"I am a regular guest on Nova."

"That's right. You're that physicist. That stuff you said about electrons behaving like particles and waves at the same time was wild, man. My mind was twisted."

"I'm glad you enjoyed it." Dave Black then turned to Professor Wagner and gave him a set of keys. "That's my spare set. Just leave them at the front desk. I'll pick them up tomorrow." He then shook all their hands again and turned his gaze back to Victoria, "I must be going now. It was nice to meet you."

After Dave Black left the building, Danny, Victoria, and Professor Wagner proceeded down a wide marble hallway with high arched ceilings while students scurried back and forth carrying backpacks and stacks of books.

Danny's legs burned and his breathing was heavy as he tried to keep up with Victoria and the professor.

They climbed an ancient marble staircase to the third floor where Professor Wagner used the keys that Dave Black had just given him to open an office door.

Inside, the office was just as elegant as the rest of the university. Polished wooden chairs surrounded an antique wooden desk and against one wall was a bookcase, full to the limit with exquisite hardcovers.

Professor Wagner exclaimed, "Dave's new office is three times bigger than mine. I should have come to California when I had the chance."

Victoria locked the door, then turned to Danny. "Show him."

With no one else to trust, Danny handed him the box.

The professor slipped on a pair of glasses and then let out a sigh that almost sounded sexual when he caressed the runes carved into the wood.

Danny was ready to explode. "What the hell is in that thing already?"

Professor Wagner glanced at Victoria, then back at Danny. "If this is what we believe it is, then you cannot see it. Just knowing it exists is enough to get you killed. If you haven't figured that out already by the Russians who almost did kill you." He slipped on a pair of surgical gloves.

"But . . . what about my dad?"

Victoria said, "We'll get your father back. But, first, this is a matter of national security. World security actually."

Professor Wagner spun around in the chair so they couldn't see what he was doing.

Danny stood.

Victoria stood and shook her head, motioning for Danny to sit back down.

He did.

CHAPTER 12

Turned around in the chair so only he could see it, Professor Wagner opened the little wooden box and found that it truly was the relic they had been searching for.

It looked like a miniature black bowling ball that had been sliced in half. When he touched the smooth black surface, it glowed blue. He had heard about it all his life but seeing it was like seeing something supernatural. It was mesmerizing. So ancient and so powerful.

He quickly closed the box and turned around in his chair. His heart was beating and his stomach was churning. Drops of perspiration formed on his forehead.

Danny and Victoria were both waiting for his response.

Professor Wagner nodded. "Finally . . . we have it."

Victoria turned to Danny and said, "Let's go down to the cafeteria. I know you're hungry."

"What about my dad?"

She replied, "I already called it in. The agency has been trying to track his cell phone. They're still trying to pinpoint his last location by the last message sent to you. There's nothing more we can do right now except wait."

Danny asked, "What if the Russians kill him?"

Professor Wagner slipped the box into his front suit jacket pocket and explained, "If you gave this box to the Russians, you and your father would both be dead already, and this little box would be on its way to Moscow."

Victoria added, "Danny, I understand your concerns, but you will have to trust us."

Danny followed Victoria and the professor out of the office and then the professor locked the door.

The professor declared, "What's in this box is more important than you can imagine. More important than any of our lives."

They headed down the hallway, which was much quieter now with only a few people here and there.

Professor Wagner thought that by telling Danny about

where the relic had come from that he could keep his mind off his kidnapped father long enough for them to get out of there and get it to a safe location. He asked, "Have you ever heard of The Ministry of Ancestry?"

Danny replied, "I don't think so. Why?"

As they headed down the stairs and then through the vast marble hallways, Professor Wagner explained, "Long before the war, there was a group of German scholars known as . . ." The professor spoke impeccable German when he said, "The *Arische Bewahrer* . . . The Aryan Preservers. They believed that all the ancient Aryan myths and stories were true and they rejected all modern religions. When Hitler took over Germany and learned of the group, he embraced them and gave them funding and a new name, The *Minissterium Abstammung,* The Ministry of Ancestry. They had spent millions traveling the world and excavating, but when Hitler had to tighten his budget due to Germany losing the war, he disbanded the group."

Everything Professor Wagner told Danny was true, except for the part about the group being disbanded. While it only consisted of a few members, the group still existed, and the professor was their highest-ranking member. He also conveniently forgot to mention that his grandfather was one of the Nazi scientists brought to America under operation paperclip to work at NASA in Texas, and that he had kept the group going through his son, Wilhelm's father, who had been an electronic engineer at Texas Instruments until he died of emphysema from smoking two packs of cigarettes a day for over thirty years. Another secret he forgot to mention was that Victoria was also a member of the group, and she was Professor Wagner's adopted daughter.

Danny asked, "If this thing is so powerful and dangerous, why didn't Hitler use it to win the war?"

Victoria stayed quiet as the three of them arrived in the spacious cafeteria that was only half full of students who were eating and studying at the same time.

Professor Wagner lowered his voice so no one else could hear what he was saying. "They didn't know how to use it . . . and they were worried about the allied forces taking possession of it, so it was kept in a safe deposit box in Switzerland. As you know . . . Switzerland was neutral throughout the war. The key was locked in a safe in a secret weapons research facility in Austria . . . the facility that your grandfather and his squad attacked and plundered."

Danny asked, "If no one could figure out how to use it, then why is it so dangerous? What the hell is it?"

The professor thought about telling Danny the rest of the story since he and Victoria were planning to kill him anyway, but he just wasn't in the mood to talk anymore. He was hungry too. "I am sorry you are frustrated, but I cannot tell you what it is."

Victoria added, "The relic is not your problem anymore. Let's just concentrate on getting your father back."

CHAPTER 13

The first thing Danny spotted in the cafeteria was the variety of cake slices under a glass display.

Victoria approached a self-serve soda machine. She handed an empty cup to Professor Wagner which he then filled with ice cubes and iced tea. She took one cup for herself, then turned to Danny and asked, "You want something to drink?" She handed him an empty cup.

Danny glanced at the selection on the machine but stuck to his favorite, regular Coke.

After topping off his cup with soda, Danny's phone beeped with a text message. He set the cup down, then checked his phone to find a text alert from his phone service provider that his payment was almost due. He deleted that message and noticed a message that he hadn't read yet. It was the last message from the Russian about breaking Danny's father's arm and killing him if he didn't give him the relic.

A tear rolled down Danny's face when he thought about his father, now old and frail, being tortured.

"Whatever that thing is. It's not worth more than my father's life." Danny showed Victoria the text.

She read it. "I told you to trust me. Now that he's texted you again, our people have a better chance of pinpointing his location."

"But this message was from eleven minutes ago. Your people should have called you by now."

Victoria glanced over at Professor Wagner.

The professor assured him, "Don't worry. Everything will be fine."

Danny knew they were patronizing him. He wanted to kick their asses and run out of there with the box. There was no chance of him overpowering Victoria, and even Professor Wagner with his perfect posture and graceful movements seemed more than formidable despite the fact that he was at least in his middle fifties.

He couldn't give up. That was another of the many reasons his ex-girlfriend gave when she dumped him, that he's a quitter.

While trying to figure out what to do, Danny turned around to face the food counter. His stomach was growling after missing his mid-morning snack as well as lunch. He felt his phone vibrate in his pocket again. When he checked it, nothing was there. He'd imagined it.

But he didn't imagine what he saw next. With his eyes still on his blackened phone screen, Danny glimpsed Victoria's reflection from behind him, pouring something into the cup of soda that he'd left sitting on the counter. When he turned around, she was placing a lid on his cup.

Victoria said, "You can't just leave something open like that. Anything could fly in there." She handed Danny the cup and smiled.

Danny took the cup, then faked a stomach pain and set the cup back down. He wanted to be vulgar to keep them from doubting him. There was no point in trying to impress Victoria anymore. "Oh shit. Those jalapenos I put in my omelet this morning are going to burn my ass now. I'll be right back." With his hand on his stomach, he hurried through the cafeteria to the back wall and then followed the restroom signs to a short hallway.

Instead of going to the end of the hall and turning left to the restrooms, he turned right, sneaking into the kitchen.

An old man in a white uniform sat on a chair with a newspaper in his hands, but he was obviously sleeping.

Danny hurried through the empty kitchen trying not to make any noise, as it would also alert the two young girls working in the adjoining counter area.

On the opposite side of the kitchen was a wide back door for deliveries. The lock was just a latch that closed from the inside.

Just as he was about to go back to the other side, he noticed one of the girls from the counter turning around and heading back toward the kitchen area. He ducked down behind some kind of machine and tried to keep his heavy breathing quiet.

The girl stopped before coming all the way back. She knelt down and pulled a phone charger from the wall and then retrieved her phone and went back up front to the counter area.

Danny checked to see that the old man was still asleep in his chair before scurrying across the kitchen to where he came in. He peeked through the tiny window in the swinging kitchen door.

Just as he was about to go out into the hall for a better look, he heard Victoria and the professor speaking. Even though he knew how ridiculous it was, Danny's natural survival instinct made him grab the biggest frying pan that was hanging on the wall.

Professor Wagner said, "I'll check the restroom. You cover the entrance in case he gets past me."

Danny couldn't see Victoria. He assumed she was going to guard the cafeteria's main entrance where they had come in from. He stood to the side, trying to spot the professor without being spotted himself.

Then he saw him. Professor Wagner turned his head toward the kitchen door. Danny pulled back, hoping the professor didn't see him—but he did.

Danny slammed the door open, hitting the professor, and making him stagger back, but he was far from being unconscious, so Danny struck his head with the frying pan, hard. A loud thump was followed by Professor Wagner falling straight down.

After glancing down the hall to make sure Victoria couldn't see him, Danny rummaged through the professor's jacket pockets and found a small leather book that was obviously very old. He opened it. Everything was handwritten and in German. Danny had no idea what it was, but it appeared to be important and valuable, so he took it. He then checked the professor's other pockets until finding the wooden box, which he held in his hand with the book and then raced through the kitchen, waking up the old man as he barreled through to the other side and then out the back entrance and into the bright sunlight.

Danny raced down the sidewalk, bumping into students as he passed them and then he dodged traffic as he bolted across the eight-lane street against the light. Cars and trucks beeped and skidded trying to avoid him.

Panting and dripping saliva from his mouth, adrenaline was the only thing that made him push harder as he sprinted into the parking structure and then up the stairs.

He fumbled for his keys while trying not to drop the wooden box and the leather book. He heard footsteps coming up the stairs, and when he turned to check it out, he dropped his keys.

Danny's hands trembled even harder as he stuffed the book and the box into his front sweatshirt pockets and then squatted down for his keys while keeping his eyes on the staircase.

He was relieved when the person going up the stairs kept going, but that relief did nothing to slow his breathing or his heart rate.

Finally, inside his car, Danny made sure the doors were locked before starting it up and skidding down the ramp.

He knew that if he saw anyone coming after him, he would have to run them down with his car. He thought about going to the cops, however, he didn't trust them either.

CHAPTER 14

The monk, Tsomo, had followed Danny and the blonde woman from Danny's father's house while staying a few cars back. He was getting the hang of freeway driving, however, he was still worried about being spotted.

When they had arrived at the university, Tsomo was surprised. He thought she would be taking Danny to a government building. She was obviously not a civilian.

He followed them into the parking structure and parked his compact beige rental car on the second level, the same level where Danny's SUV was parked, on the opposite side.

He didn't have a direct line of sight from where he was parked, but a large round mirror hanging on the concrete wall provided a reflection he could use. He just hoped they didn't notice him.

Tsomo stayed low in the driver's seat while Danny and the woman left the structure on foot.

Without getting out of the car, he quickly changed into the clothes left by his contact. A pair of white sneakers, blue jeans, and a zip-up hooded sweatshirt, all new, and all a perfect fit. He didn't like hats, but the blue Dodger's hat changed his appearance drastically, so he used it.

Standing along the side wall, Tsomo stepped toward an opening and peered outside.

Danny and the woman crossed the street and entered the university building while people on the sidewalks and cars on the streets zipped back and forth.

He wanted to follow them inside, but he was worried about losing them in there, so he stayed in the parking structure, watching the street.

Tsomo finally received a message about the location of the relic. It was right across the street in the university. At least he knew he was on the right track.

While standing there, watching the building, Tsomo hoped the woman didn't take the relic and leave without Danny. It had taken him so long to get its location. He couldn't afford to lose it now.

He considered the vast building across the street. There was no way he could find them in there now. They could be on any floor. And the building took up the whole block. Tsomo's only choice was to wait. He used his meditation skills to calm his nerves and slow his breathing.

Finally, after what seemed like hours, he spotted Danny running down the sidewalk alone and then crossing the street, almost getting hit by traffic.

Tsomo moved out of the way when Danny glanced up.

He didn't see anyone running after him, yet he assumed Danny was running from someone.

Tsomo ducked back down into his rental car and wondered if he should just take the relic from Danny right there in the parking lot, but he knew there were cameras everywhere, and he also knew that blonde woman couldn't be too far, and she was armed. He could easily get away from them there, however, he still had to get the relic out of the country, and Tibet was a long way from California.

Doubting himself the entire time, Tsomo decided to wait. He would follow Danny and approach him in a better place, and hopefully, the relic would be in Danny's possession. Why else would he be running?

He watched as Danny fumbled to get into his SUV and then after easing out of his parking spot, he sped down the ramp.

Wondering how long would be too long to wait, Tsomo started up his car, then cruised slowly down the ramp, still checking both ways for the blonde woman or anyone else who seemed out of place.

CHAPTER 15

Professor Wagner woke up with a sharp pain in his head and a throbbing headache. It took him a couple of minutes to realize that he was on the floor next to the university cafeteria kitchen.

He remembered seeing Danny through the tiny window in the swinging kitchen door, but he didn't remember anything after that.

Before trying to stand, he checked his pocket to find that the box was missing. He then realized the book was also missing.

Victoria approached. "What happened?"

"He took the box . . . and the journal." The professor struggled while trying to stand.

Victoria stopped him.

By that time, a few students were leering at them.

"Don't move." She glanced at his forehead. "He hit you with something. You may have a concussion. Do you know who I am?"

"Of course I know who you are."

Victoria moved her hand back and forth in front of his face as he followed it with his eyes. She said, "If it were me lying there you would be worried about the same thing."

"Okay, okay. You are Victoria. I am Wilhelm Wagner." He counted to ten quickly, forward and backward, then he tried to stand again while ignoring the ringing in his ears. "I don't have a concussion."

She helped him the rest of the way up and then led him into the kitchen.

The old man in white was filling a sink with water. He turned to them when they entered. "Hey. You're not supposed to be in here."

They ignored him while crossing through the kitchen and then outside through the open service door.

"Hey!" The old man raised his voice. "Who opened that door?"

Standing on the sidewalk, under the bright sun, watching cars and pedestrians go by, Professor Wagner asked, "How long was I out?"

"Not more than a few minutes. He couldn't have gotten far." She then typed something into her phone and stared at the screen. "I'm not seeing him anywhere. He must have taken the battery out of his phone."

The professor's headache was getting worse. He rubbed his temples, disappointed with himself. "You're going to have to drive."

They retrieved his rental car, which was a big black Chevy Tahoe.

After climbing into the Tahoe and adjusting the seat and mirrors, Victoria typed their destination into her phone and then followed the directions to the nearest freeway.

Professor Wagner thought about the ancient Vedic story of when *Goutama* tricked *Manikundala*, then he remembered that *Manikundala* had been victorious in the end. The ancient myths always comforted him. As a child, he grew up hearing the mythological stories from his grandfather, and while Professor Wagner had his PhD in physics, he also held a master's degree in linguistics, which was inspired by his love for the myths and his desire to obtain more knowledge of the ancient Aryans.

CHAPTER 16

Detective Robertson finally received a report on the corpse they had found at Daniel Ackerman, Sr.'s house. It was a John Doe. No fingerprints in the system and no identification of any kind. The only thing they knew for sure was the make and the caliber of the bullets that they had dug out of his skull.

He hoped the senior homicide detective would be getting out of court before the sheriff or the state police decided to show up and make him look like a fool.

On one hand, Robertson felt as if he should be able to solve the case on his own. And if it was a conventional murder, he probably could have. But on the other hand, he knew this was a complicated case as the dead man was obviously no street thug and the owner of the house was still missing. The only fingerprints in the house belonged to Daniel Ackerman, and his son Danny. There was no evidence that Danny or his father had even been there when John Doe was killed.

Robertson glanced at the picture of his family on his desk. His wife had been trying to build up his confidence and he felt like he'd be letting her down if he failed. He also didn't want to have to tell his kids that Daddy couldn't catch the bad guy.

CHAPTER 17

Danny had gone to the mission at San Juan Capistrano as a child on a school field trip. He remembered a deteriorating old church, a bunch of boring museum exhibits, and something about birds. The only thing on his mind back then was a cute little brunette who he had long forgotten the name of, and the recent release of PlayStation Two, which at the time, he wanted more than the girl.

When he arrived, he parked across the street in an open parking lot that was less than half full.

Founded in 1776 by Spanish Catholics of the Franciscan Order, the mission was a complex of one and two-story beige stucco buildings with open brick archways all the way around. Red terracotta roofs featured turrets topped with crosses while palm trees and colorful flower gardens adorned the grounds.

A group of tourists followed their guide while she explained the history of the mission. A few other tourists were on their own, taking pictures with their phones as well as with zoom lens cameras.

Danny glanced across the street at the main entrance and realized he had to pay admission. He was running out of money fast. He only had a few dollars to begin with, and he still hadn't eaten lunch yet. His stomach was growling.

After snapping the battery back into his phone, Danny found another text message that instructed him to go inside the basilica. He knew he was taking a chance by keeping his phone on, but he didn't know where the basilica was, and he didn't want to waste time trying to find out, so he googled it and then took the battery back out of his phone once he knew where to go.

The basilica was on the opposite side of the mission, and fortunately, he didn't have to pay to get in.

Danny took the wooden box and the little book and stuffed them into his front sweatshirt pockets.

Scanning the area to be sure Victoria hadn't found him,

he hurried along the sidewalk past the mission buildings and then finally up a short set of steps to a square white church with a bell tower and a cross on top. Both sets of ornate double doors were open.

CHAPTER 18

Although Professor Wagner and Victoria had lost Danny at the university, they knew from the text message he had shown them that he was going to the mission at San Juan Capistrano.

Victoria was driving the big black Tahoe while the professor rubbed his temples in a futile attempt at relieving his throbbing headache.

When they arrived, Victoria pointed at the burgundy SUV in the parking lot across the street from the mission. "There's his car."

"Can you see if he's in it?"

"I can't tell from here." She stopped at the red light and waited. Finally, the light turned green and she proceeded forward and then into the parking lot.

Professor Wagner squinted as they approached Danny's SUV. "I don't think he's in there."

Victoria stopped the Tahoe and jumped out with her pistol down at her side. She peeked into Danny's windows and said, "Nope. He's not here."

The professor noticed a man that could have been Danny entering the square white basilica on the opposite side of the mission. "I believe we have him."

Victoria turned and asked, "Where?"

"If that was him . . . he just entered that church."

Victoria climbed back into the Tahoe and shifted it into drive. She pulled out of the parking lot and onto the street while the professor kept his eye on the open basilica doors.

Victoria slowed down and asked, "Are you sure that was him?"

"No." Replied Professor Wagner. "Not one hundred percent." He glanced out the back window and said, "But it looked like him . . . and his car hasn't moved."

"I'm going to circle around." Victoria waited for another red light to turn green, then she made the turn and followed the street around the back of the basilica where they found another set of ornate double doors, but they were closed.

The professor said, "I wonder if those doors are unlocked. Wait here. I'll check."

"Hurry. We don't want to miss him if he goes back out the other side." Victoria pulled over alongside a row of parked cars and turned on the flashing hazard lights.

Professor Wagner jumped out and approached the basilica doors as cars on the street slowed down and beeped their horns while going around the double-parked Tahoe.

Both sets of doors were locked.

CHAPTER 19

Alex had been sitting in the basilica for about ten minutes admiring the tall gray and white arches. The wall behind the altar featured a statue of Jesus on top, Mary below Jesus, and two apostles on each side.

He stared at Jesus on the cross and asked forgiveness for Ingrid then he silently recited a Russian prayer he'd learned from his grandmother when he was just a boy.

While the churches in Russia were much flashier with their gold walls and crystal chandeliers, Alex felt that this less flamboyant style depicted Christianity better.

A few people sat in silence here and there as others knelt and whispered prayers.

Alex didn't want to keep turning around, so he positioned himself at an angle at the end of the pew, giving him a partial view of the open front doors and the bright sun outside.

Finally, when Danny arrived, Alex stood and raised his hand so Danny could see him, then he sank back down onto the pew and pretended to stare ahead at Jesus.

Danny approached and eyeballed Alex.

"Hello, Danny." He slid over on the pew making room for him. "Sit down."

Danny took a seat next to him and asked, "Where's my dad?"

"He's in a car. A few minutes away from here. Once I have the relic in my hand, I'll make the call and someone will bring your father here and set him free."

"How do I know I can trust you?"

With his gaze fixed on the statue of Jesus, Alex asked, "Are you a religious man?"

"Not really," Replied Danny.

"Well, that's too bad. Because now you will need to have faith." Alex stared into Danny's eyes and commanded, "Give me the relic."

Danny hesitated, then he removed the little wooden box

from his sweatshirt pocket and gave it to Alex.

Alex opened the box and his heart almost stopped when he realized what he was holding. Just that morning, his superiors told him the story of the relic and how it ended up in America. At first, Alex wondered if he was just chasing a myth since no Russian had actually ever seen it before, but now, there was no doubt.

CHAPTER 20

For the first time since it had been in his possession, Danny finally saw what was in the box.

Alex held it in his hand and ogled it. He had the same expression on his face that Professor Wagner had.

It seemed like nothing to Danny. A small, smooth, black sphere that had been sliced in half. "You kidnapped my dad and destroyed his house for that? What the hell is it?"

Alex replied, "Just try to forget you ever saw it. Or I will be forced to retract my compassion."

"Compassion?"

"Yes. Compassion. I am letting you and your father live when I could easily have you both killed right now. That's compassion."

Danny kept his mouth shut, hoping his dad was okay. The marijuana edible was just beginning to kick in while his empty stomach continued to growl. He started sweating.

Alex texted something on his phone, waited a moment for a return text, then he stood and said, "He's on his way."

He had never mentioned the little leather book so Danny assumed Alex didn't know anything about it, or he just didn't know that Danny had it. Either way, he wasn't going to volunteer the information.

Danny followed Alex outside.

Stepping out of the dark basilica and into the bright sunlight was blinding. While standing on the white concrete steps, Danny's eyes adjusted.

He noticed a black Mercedes with tinted windows coming toward them and when he strained to see inside the car, he only saw one man—the driver, another Russian with a mean face.

Danny's heart pounded. He thought he had been tricked and they were going to kill him anyway.

Just when he considered making a run for it, the Mercedes got closer and Danny could see a silhouette in the back seat, staring out the tinted window.

"Is that my dad in the back?"
Alex nodded.
Danny exhaled.

CHAPTER 21

When the next traffic light turned green, Victoria circled around the back of the basilica in the Tahoe.

Professor Wagner said, "There's a parking lot over there, with a clear line of sight to the basilica."

"But we'll be too far away if we have to make a move on foot."

As Victoria cruised by, the professor noticed Danny and Alex coming out of the basilica. "There. The kid and the Russian. Ten to one the Russians have it. They probably killed the father already."

"Only if the kid was dumb enough to give up the relic without seeing his father first. But, I don't think so."

Professor Wagner said, "You sound like you admire the kid."

"Admire? No. But I have to admit . . . he certainly surprised me. And he did get the best of *us*."

"Don't remind me." Rubbing his head, the professor turned back to look out the window and assess the situation. "We should take them both out while we have the chance."

"In front of a church? There are witnesses everywhere. Did you forget that we're trying to avoid attention?" Victoria slowed down as she passed Danny and Alex.

A black Mercedes slowed as it approached the basilica.

Professor Wagner noticed an Asian man in a sweatshirt and a blue Dodgers cap sneaking up behind Danny and Alex on the sidewalk.

CHAPTER 22

Tsomo was there when Danny entered the basilica and he had been waiting for him to come out.

As soon as he saw the Russian next to Danny and the expression on both of their faces, he knew that Danny was no longer in possession of the relic.

With no more time to waste, Tsomo crept up behind the Russian and struck him in the back of the neck, at the top of the spine. One single precise blow.

Instantly, the Russian fell to the ground, unconscious.

Two old women who were coming out of the basilica screamed and stepped back inside when they saw Tsomo attack the Russian.

A black Mercedes that was pulling up to the curb suddenly peeled out and sped away, zigzagging through traffic and then speeding through a red light and almost hitting a black Chevy Tahoe as cars skidded out of the way and beeped their horns.

Danny yelled, "No!"

Tsomo snatched the little wooden box from the Russian on the ground and then he pulled Danny by the shirt and made him go with him around the side of the basilica where his compact beige rental car was waiting with the engine running.

He didn't force Danny into the car. Instead, he said, "Without the mind, you are worth nothing to them. They will kill you now. Come with me if you value your life."

CHAPTER 23

Professor Wagner had his eyes on Danny and Alex in front of the basilica when he noticed the Asian man attack Alex, but before he could tell Victoria, a black Mercedes that was pulling up to the curb had sped away and came right toward them. Fortunately, Victoria spun the wheel just in time, swerving, and avoiding the collision. The Mercedes kept going, almost causing another accident as it sped through the red light.

Victoria asked, "Follow them?"

"No." Professor Wagner pointed in the direction of the basilica. "A monk just knocked out the Russian and the kid went with him."

She slowed down and then made a dangerous and illegal U-turn as cars swerved to avoid hitting her.

The professor said, "That side . . . they were on foot."

Victoria made another turn and then followed the smaller street around the front of the basilica until they were back on the side where they had started.

Professor Wagner looked around for Danny and the monk. "If the monks are helping him . . ."

She made another U-turn. This time the professor wasn't expecting it. He held on as gravity pushed him back in his seat. Once they were going straight again, he asked, "You see them?"

Victoria pulled into the parking lot. Danny's SUV was still parked there, yet there was no sign of him.

Professor Wagner rubbed his head, which was pounding even worse.

Victoria cruised slowly through the parking lot, circling Danny's SUV.

CHAPTER 24

When Alex opened his eyes, his vision was blurry and his memories were confused. When he saw the palm trees above, he thought of Israel and Ingrid, but then the sights and sounds around him reminded him that he was in California, at the mission at San Juan Capistrano.

As the blurriness began to fade, he could make out the figure standing above him. It was a cop.

The cop instructed, "Try not to move, sir. An ambulance is on the way."

Alex noticed two old women standing inside the basilica watching and trembling. He turned back to the cop. "I don't need an ambulance. I'm fine." Alex felt dizzy when he stood. If his embassy received a call from the hospital, then his superiors would find out that he had failed.

The cop continued trying to convince Alex to stay down, but Alex made it to his feet. He knew the relic would be gone. He checked his pockets to find that he still had his wallet, so he opened it and showed the cop his ID. "They didn't even take my money. Probably just a crazy person."

He brushed off his expensive suit and proclaimed, "Thank god they didn't hurt my suit."

The cop explained, "The women here said you were with someone."

Alex turned to the women who averted their gaze from him and then he turned back to the cop and replied, "Some kid approached me. They must have been working together. They were probably planning to rob me. Thank god these two women were here. Who knows what those lunatics could have done to me." He smiled at the old women who were obviously confused.

CHAPTER 25

While sitting next to Tsomo as he drove painfully slow on the busy freeway, Danny said, "You were at the hospital this morning . . . wearing a red robe."

"Correct. I am Tsomo."

"Well Tsomo . . . those Russians have my dad . . . and they're probably going to kill him now because you took what they wanted."

"No man shall know the mind of Krishna."

"You said that shit at the hospital. I didn't know what you meant then and I don't know what you mean now. Just give me back my property so I can go get my dad back. They're going to kill him. Don't you care?"

"What is in this box is not your property. It belongs to no mortal man. And yes . . . to answer your question . . . I do care . . . I always care when living beings are made to suffer."

"Do you always talk like this? What the fuck? And why are you driving so slow?"

Tsomo cruised down an off-ramp and then followed a street with shopping centers and gas stations on both sides until turning down a skinny side street and then parking in a lot just off the corner, next to a motel. "Please excuse my English. Someone will translate for me."

"I understand you just fine. Just give me back my grandpa's box." That was the first time Danny had considered the fact that they may have come for his grandfather. "Oh, shit. I have to call my grandpa to see if he's okay."

Tsomo exited the car and approached a room on the lower level of the motel.

Danny felt like just punching him out and taking the box. Maybe there was still time to save his father. But of course, he knew that if he tried to put his hands on Tsomo he'd get his ass kicked. He remembered how easily the little man took down Alex, with just a single strike. Danny wasn't taking any chances.

After opening the door, Tsomo turned to Danny and said, "Please. Come in."

"You better not try any gay shit with me." Danny hesitated before going all the way inside.

It was a typical motel room with two twin beds, faded carpets, and a TV bolted to the wall.

There was one thing that wasn't typical. He wondered if the marijuana candy he'd had earlier was causing him to have an LSD flashback from his younger years. Danny's fifth-grade teacher was there. A chubby Asian woman in her sixties with shoulder-length black and gray hair, and a round face. Other than the obvious aging, she looked exactly as he remembered her, wearing a pair of thick glasses, a long brown skirt that covered even her feet, and a beige blouse with a red and green flower pattern. Miss Stong.

"Surprise." Exclaimed Miss Stong.

Tsomo closed the motel room door, then entered the bathroom and closed that door.

Miss Stong said, "I guess you're wondering why I'm here."

"Um . . . yeah. I mean . . . yeah."

"Tsomo is my cousin. My family is responsible for that thing everyone has been chasing. We knew your grandfather brought it here from Europe, but we couldn't locate its signal. We knew he must have had it in a bank or a safe somewhere all these years."

Danny's stomach growled and Miss Stong must have heard it because she took some items out of a plastic shopping bag and placed them onto the desk. Cans of soda and bottles of water. Fruits, crackers, nuts, and chocolate.

He went right for the chocolate.

She then opened another plastic bag and took out a plastic container. "Rice and vegetables." She took out another container. "I know it's probably not your favorite, but you are welcome to have some."

"Thank you." Danny washed down the chocolate with

some soda and then opened the rice. She was right. It wasn't his favorite, but he was so hungry, and now that he'd had his sugar, his body was craving nutrients.

Miss Stong then opened a duffle bag, took out a few sets of clothing and a stack of cash, and threw them onto one of the beds.

Tsomo returned from the bathroom and scarfed down his rice and vegetables as if it were his last meal.

Danny thought about that phrase and hoped it wasn't an omen.

In between stuffing his face with the healthiest meal he'd had in years, Danny said, "If my grandpa had it in his possession all this time . . . then it's his now. Come on . . . seventy years? Finders keepers. And anyways, I need it to get my dad back before those Russians kill him."

Tsomo swallowed the food in his mouth and then replied, "No mortal life is worth the mind of Krishna. But do not fret . . . your father's sacrifice will be rewarded in his next life."

"His next life? I'm getting really tired of this Hare Krishna bullshit. My father's life is worth more than yours, you fucking dickhead." Danny threw the rest of his rice into Tsomo's face.

Tsomo was on his feet instantly, ready to strike.

Miss Stong spoke in their language.

Without any expression on his face, Tsomo behaved like a robot. He lowered his hands to his sides and then bowed to Danny, then after wiping the food off his face, he sat back down and continued eating as if nothing had happened.

While cleaning up the mess, Miss Stong warned, "My cousin can kill you with a touch. I suggest you do not provoke him again."

Danny didn't care. He was feeling defiant. He showed both of his middle fingers to Tsomo and taunted him. "Fuck you. Fucking dickhead."

Tsomo ignored him and continued eating.

CHAPTER 26

Still sitting at his desk, staring at the notes he had made on the case and wishing he had more to go on, Detective Robertson considered going back to the scene of the crime, then he decided to wait for his partner, the senior homicide detective, to arrive. He had already tried calling him, but he didn't answer. Robertson knew he was still in court so he left a voicemail that he needed help.

Just as he was about to get up and get a bottle of water from the refrigerator in the break room, a stunning blonde woman with piercing blue eyes and a black skirt suit entered the room.

Other cops turned to gawk at her when she came in, and most of them stared at her as she sashayed past their desks.

She approached the last desk and asked, "Are you Detective Robertson?"

Robertson had never cheated on his wife, but at that moment, while admiring the athletic physique and generous breasts that her buttoned-to-the-top blouse couldn't hide, and inhaling the heavenly aroma of her perfume, he considered it. "Yes. I'm Detective Robertson." He cleared his throat and asked, "How can I be of assistance?"

She showed her CIA credentials and spoke with a commanding voice. "Agent Becker. I need everything you have on the Ackerman case."

He handed her the folder and admitted, "I don't have much, Victoria."

"I prefer you call me Agent Becker." She scanned the forensics reports as well as Robertson's notes and then instructed, "Print out a copy of Daniel Ackerman Junior's arrest records."

Robertson asked, "His son? You think he could have killed that man with two perfect shots to the head? And who trashed the house? They were searching for something. That much is obvious."

"Please don't try to think, Detective. Just print out the

records. I also need all records of anyone Danny had been arrested with in the past. No matter how long ago."

Her attitude made Robertson get an attitude of his own, yet he was still attracted to her, maybe even more. He bowed his head and said, "Your wish is my command, your highness."

Victoria's face was as cold and flawless as an ice statue. No emotions or reactions whatsoever. She used her phone to take pictures of the documents in the folder, then she glanced up at Robertson, who had pulled up Danny's records on his computer.

Robertson explained, "He was arrested once . . . for being drunk in public and disturbing the peace . . . that was seven years ago on his twenty-first birthday. Two of his friends were also arrested with him." He printed out the report and then handed it to Victoria.

She scanned the arrest report and then instructed, "I need all the information you can find on the two friends who were arrested with him. Addresses. Arrest records. Everything and anything."

While typing their names into his computer, Robertson asked, "So . . . how does your husband feel about you being CIA? I mean . . . can't that get dangerous? Especially for such a beautiful woman."

Victoria answered his question with a question of her own. "Is that your wife and kids in that picture? How does she feel about you being a cop? That can be dangerous too."

He knew she was just trying to put him in his place. And it worked. "Yes. She worries."

CHAPTER 27

Once back in his motel room near the university, Professor Wagner finally had a chance to take a couple of Advil and lie down. He wanted to sleep, but he promised Victoria he wouldn't. She was still worried he could have a concussion. He massaged his temples while listening to classical music from the clock radio on the night table next to him.

He was just beginning to doze off when Victoria entered the room. His eyes jolted open.

After placing the police files onto the bed next to him, she headed into the bathroom.

Professor Wagner sat up, quickly read the arrest reports, and then asked loudly, "I guess your plan is to look for him at one of his friend's houses?"

Born in Texas, Victoria's young parents died when a stage collapsed at a rock concert. Victoria was less than a year old and was at her babysitter's house when the tragedy occurred. With no responsible family willing to take her, Victoria was raised in an orphanage until she was six years old. The professor and his wife couldn't have children so they adopted Victoria after learning of her ultra-high intelligence. He eventually told Victoria about the secret society he belonged to, now renamed *The Aryan Preservers*. And then he groomed her by sending her to the US Air Force and college and then getting her to apply at the CIA.

She had been working with the CIA for a few years but was not a field operative. She wasn't even sure if she ever would be. There weren't many of them. As of now, she was officially on vacation.

Professor Wagner kept it to himself, but he was worried about the trouble she could get into if her superiors at the CIA found out what she was doing.

Finally, Victoria came out of the bathroom and perched herself onto the edge of the other bed.

Professor Wagner declared, "We will find him and we

will punish him like Zeus punished Sisyphus for believing that he was so clever he could outsmart the gods."

"The only problem with that is . . . we're not gods."

"No . . . but we were chosen by the gods." The professor yawned, then lay back on the bed and said, "Now that you're here to keep an eye on me, I'd like to try to sleep off some of this headache."

Victoria replied, "Thirty minutes."

"Yes, *Heerführer*."

Victoria smirked and said, "Go to sleep."

He closed his eyes. His head was spinning as everything that had happened that day replayed in his memory, over and over.

CHAPTER 28

When Alex finally returned to the boarded-up old bookstore where his accomplice had Daniel, Sr. tied to a chair, he was furious and he had to take it out on someone. He didn't really break his arm earlier, that was just a bluff, but now, Alex was ready to inflict some pain. But not too much because he needed the old man to be able to flee at a moment's notice.

Alex punched Daniel, Sr. in the face, twice, as his Russian accomplice stood silently at attention.

Daniel, Sr. choked on his gag as snot dripped from his nose and he hyperventilated.

Alex felt better, but not a hundred percent better. He felt like punching him again, so he did.

Daniel, Sr. struggled against the ropes that were holding him to the chair.

When Alex finally removed the gag, blood and saliva dripped from the old man's mouth as he coughed and gasped for air. A tooth fell out of his mouth, bounced off his belly, and landed on the bloody floor.

Alex asked, "Who is helping your son?"

Daniel, Sr. replied in barely more than a whisper, "I don't know."

"I believe you." Alex punched him in the stomach.

He gasped for air, then, when he was finally able to speak again, he asked, "If you believe me . . . then why did you hit me again?"

"I'd like to hit your son . . . but he's not here." Alex pointed at the silent Russian standing at attention and said, "I'm certainly not going to hit *him*." Alex took a swig of vodka from a flask and then stuffed the gag back into Daniel, Sr.'s mouth.

Not sure if Danny would get it, Alex was planning to send him a text anyway. Not from his father's phone which he had already destroyed, but from his own phone.

Included with the message that read this was his last

chance, was a photo of Danny's dad tied up, gagged, and bloody. Even though he thought it would probably be too small to see on a phone screen, he held the camera at an angle so the tooth on the floor would be visible.

Alex then took another swig and worried.

He had never failed a mission, and he wasn't about to start now. There was no way of him locating Danny or the monk who had helped him. He just hoped having Danny's father would be enough to lure them to him.

CHAPTER 29

Tsomo had never been so exhausted. He hadn't had any serious sleep in a couple of days, but he had been trained for that. This wasn't his first time staying awake for days at a time. Maybe it was the mental stress of finding the relic while at the same time a lack of meditation that was draining his energy.

He understood why Danny was angry with him. He thought of him as an obstacle when it came to getting his father back. However, Tsomo couldn't make Danny understand how important the relic was without giving up all of its secrets. He lay down on the bed and listened as Danny asked his cousin, Miss Stong, a million questions.

She told him just what he needed to know about the relic. "It cannot be destroyed, and it cannot fall into the hands of men. It must be returned to its original resting place. A place no mortal man can know of."

"Except the monks." Added Danny.

Miss Stong replied, "The monks are the guardians, chosen by the god, Krishna, to guard his secret from mankind."

"I don't understand. What do Krishna and those gods have to do with Nazi technology?"

Without opening his eyes, Tsomo proclaimed, "Your pursuit of knowledge is admirable . . . but this secret you shall never know, young Daniel."

Danny turned to Miss Stong and asked, "Who does he think he is? Yoda or something?"

Tsomo's head felt heavier with each passing second. The relic was in his possession, and it would finally be returned after all these years. Knowing that everything was falling into place, he gave up fighting it and allowed himself to drift into a deep sleep.

CHAPTER 30

Miss Stong giggled when Tsomo began to snore, then, she yawned.

Danny had slipped a heavy dose of edible marijuana into both of their food earlier. It had taken longer than he'd hoped, but they were finally beginning to feel its effects. It was three times as much as he would have taken and he'd been smoking weed since high school. He knew it would be enough to knock them out, he just hoped it wasn't too much. He didn't care about Tsomo, but Miss Stong had been his favorite teacher growing up.

She yawned again and then opened another bottle of water and downed the whole thing before lying back on the second bed and closing her eyes. "I'm not used to running around like this. I'm just going to close my eyes for a minute."

Danny was almost ready to make his move. He waited a few more minutes until he was sure Miss Stong was sleeping, then he slipped the battery back into his phone to check for any messages from the Russians. His stomach twisted when he saw the picture of his father tied up and bloody. Tears filled his eyes.

He crept toward the bed Miss Stong was lying on and took the stack of cash. He stood there for a moment, hoping the edibles kept Tsomo knocked out so he couldn't hear how hard and fast his heart was beating.

The box was in Tsomo's hand, which was now partially open as he snored.

As Danny crept closer, his heart beat faster. When he reached out for the box in Tsomo's hand, it reminded him of the game, Operation. Just as he was about to snatch it, Tsomo snored harder and moved slightly.

Sweating and trembling, Danny glanced over at Miss Stong. She was out cold.

Danny made his move. He reached out, grasped the box, and then slowly pulled it away from Tsomo's hand while trying not to touch him.

With the box and the cash in his possession, Danny took the rental car keys from the desk and opened the door slowly while his heart almost exploded out of his chest.

Once outside, he closed the door gently and then raced to Tsomo's rental car in the parking lot.

The sun was on its way down, but the streetlamps weren't on yet.

Even while starting the car, he was worried Tsomo would wake up and take him out with some of that Shaolin shit he did back at the basilica.

Fortunately, there was no sign of Tsomo or Miss Stong.

Danny laughed out loud while driving away and recalling how he left them there snoring. He turned on the radio and said, "Dickhead," and laughed again.

Danny didn't know if Tsomo would report the rental car stolen, so he didn't want to keep it too long, just in case. He considered going to the mission to get his own car back, but then he thought about everyone else who was after him and gave up on that idea. He couldn't even go home to feed his cats and see if they were okay. And of course, he knew people would be at the hospital watching grandpa. His dad's two-year-old Buick was in the garage, but going back to his dad's house was also no longer an option.

With nowhere else to go, Danny decided to contact his ex-girlfriend, Gracie.

He drove Tsomo's rental car to a supermarket and then parked in the busy parking lot. He left the car there and then trekked for ten minutes through a quiet residential neighborhood.

Gracie worked full-time as a veterinarian's assistant while going to school part-time to become a veterinarian herself.

Danny knew that the old man who had hired her and promised to keep her working after she finished her degree, had a crush on her. He told her that many times, yet she refused to believe it. She said he's a kind old man with children older than her who just needed another vet to take up some of the hours at the animal clinic as he got closer to retirement. Danny explained that the old man could be genuinely kind, but that didn't mean he didn't want to sleep with her. She told Danny he was just being jealous.

That wasn't her only complaint about their relationship, but it was the straw that broke the camel's back.

Danny knew that Gracie had taken over the evening hours in the clinic so the old man could spend more time at home with his wife. He also knew that the old man stayed late at the clinic on more than one occasion, but of course, that was just more of Danny being jealous and insecure. He just hoped the old man wasn't there now.

The animal clinic was in between a pet store and a liquor store in a shopping center that was separated from the street by a parking lot. The pet store was closed and the steakhouse on the corner was the busiest place there.

Danny stood in the park across the street as young children played soccer on the field behind him, their parents watching from the sidelines. The streetlights came on as the sun continued its descent. From where he stood, he could see perfectly into the veterinarian's office.

While watching Gracie in her pink smock, Danny thought back to all the evenings that she had come over after work and removed a smock just like that one before inviting him into the shower with her.

Gracie was tall and thick with a pretty face, lustrous reddish-blonde hair, exquisite breasts, and a healthy sex drive. Danny missed her, especially her hearty laugh. He tried to convince her to take him back after she dumped him a couple of months ago, but she refused. He even tried begging. That didn't work either.

Danny was happy with the way their relationship was. He enjoyed staying at home with a good movie and some popcorn from the microwave, but Gracie wanted to go out more than she wanted to stay in. She didn't like weed, and she always said that it made him lazy and unmotivated.

He hated to blame the weed because he enjoyed it so much, however, deep down inside he knew it wasn't helping. Over the years he had enrolled in, started, and then quit many things, including auto mechanics school, bartender's school, and even big rig truck driving school. He was genuinely interested in those things when he had enrolled, but when he realized the work involved, he just got lazy, and two out of three of those times it had cost him a lot of money.

Gracie typed something on a computer and then she entered the back room.

Danny scoped out the area. He didn't see anyone suspicious, but with the people he was running from, he knew he would never see them coming.

Worried about getting Gracie involved, Danny was about to walk away, but he had no other place to go.

The police would probably just give him over to the CIA, who already tried to slip something into his drink. Even if it wasn't meant to kill him, Danny didn't like drugs that he didn't administer himself.

He pulled his hood up over his head and then when the traffic light turned green, he crossed the street as quickly as possible without running and then stepped between two SUV's parked in the parking lot.

Instead of waiting for Gracie to return from the back, he hurried into the clinic, through the office area, and then into the back room where the animal cages and operating tables were.

It was the first time he'd been back there. White walls, cabinets, machines, and medical equipment made it seem like a real hospital.

When Gracie saw Danny with his hood covering most of his face, she put her hands up and exclaimed, "We don't keep cash here." She was about to say something else, but then she stepped closer to him. "Danny?"

Danny removed his hood.

With her hand over her heart, Gracie exclaimed, "What

the hell are you doing?" She punched him in the shoulder.

"I had to be sure no one was following me."

"Oh my god. Don't tell me—"

Gracie had a cousin who was a heavy cocaine user, and every time he got high, he thought people were following him. Danny knew by the expression on her face, that's what she was thinking about him now. He assured her, "I'm not paranoid, and I'm not high. This is for real." He took the wooden box and the leather book from his front sweatshirt pocket and showed them to her. "The Russian's took my dad. The CIA tried to slip something in my drink. And then the monk . . . my fifth grade teacher is his cousin . . . I just barely got away from them—"

Gracie interrupted him, "Did you take acid again? I should get you to a hospital."

"I didn't take anything." Danny slipped the box and the book back into his pocket then took out his phone and battery. "I can only put the battery in for a second. Or they will track me." He could tell she thought he'd lost his mind, but he had to show her the only evidence he had. Once the battery was in, he waited for the phone to start up. Finally, he showed Gracie the picture of his dad tied up and bloody.

"Oh my god." Gracie read the message that came with the picture, then she zoomed in and asked, "Is that his tooth on the ground?"

"What? Where?" Danny zoomed in all the way and when he saw it, he began to cry.

Gracie placed her hand on his wrist.

Danny texted a reply to the message: *I have what you want. I will give it to you. Do not hurt my dad.*

CHAPTER 31

By the time he got Danny's text message, Alex already had a few shots of vodka in him, so he decided it would be better to wait until morning. He left Danny's dad at the boarded-up bookstore with his men and then went home to eat and shower.

The Russian government paid for his apartment, which was on the second floor of an apartment complex that featured a pool and a community clubhouse.

His furniture wasn't fancy, but it was all brand new. Alex knew that after this mission, whether successful or not, that he'd most likely be leaving the United States.

When he considered all the places he'd been, his thoughts once again returned to Ingrid. Alex downed two more shots of vodka, but that didn't wash away the memories of her green eyes or her soft touch.

He thought back to those times:

Ingrid was three years older than Alex. They both came from KGB families and they were both Russian spies.

Posing as a married couple, they had traveled to Paris on a mission to assassinate a news reporter who allegedly had proof of the Russian government's direct involvement in mafia money laundering.

The job was easy. The seller arrived first. It wasn't hard for Ingrid with her creamy long legs and silky black hair to convince the seller that she was sent by the buyer and that she was to take him to a hotel room where she had the money. She pushed him into the back of a taxi and stuck a needle in his neck so fast he didn't have time to open his mouth before he was unconscious. When the driver glanced back, she told him the man was drunk. She paid him and sent him to a fake address on the other side of the city.

Alex's job was even easier, carrying a manila envelope that contained blank sheets of printer paper, he stood next to the buyer at the bar and then he motioned for the man to follow him, which he did. Inside the restroom, he handed the man the envelope, and when the man reached for it, Alex injected him in the hand. Within seconds, the man was on the bathroom floor and Alex was gone.

He and Ingrid quickly traveled to Amsterdam by train and then to England by ferry. When they spent the night in London, they had sex for the first time. It wasn't like sex with anyone else. It was sensual but savage at the same time. They slept all night in each other's arms, and then they did it again in the morning.

Once they were back outside, they were professionals again. The Russian government would never condone a relationship between two of their spies, and they could possibly be killed for it.

Ingrid wanted to go to a famous spa while they were in London, so Alex took advantage of that time to go clothes shopping.

Weeks later, his superiors in Moscow grilled him about their time in London. When they were convinced Alex wasn't a traitor to his country, they told him that Ingrid was. He refused to believe it. They told him that she had booked a trip to Israel and that she was working for both the Israeli's and the English.

Alex refused to believe it.

Ingrid had told him she was going to visit her sick aunt in St. Petersburg.

Alex's superiors provided him with a ticket to Israel and the location where she was staying.

The first thing he noticed in Israel was the palm trees. The trees he'd seen in movies as a child and always wanted to see up close. He even touched one on his way into the beachfront hotel where Ingrid was supposedly staying.

At the front desk, he asked for her using two different names, names he knew she had passports for. When he learned that she was staying there, his heart almost stopped. He asked the girl at the counter to call her room, and when the girl turned around to make the call, he glanced at the room number on the computer screen and then he slipped out of sight and into an elevator.

In the hall, outside of someone's door, was a covered tray. Alex lifted the cover to find an unfinished plate of food. He wiped off the dirty steak knife, then held it down at his side in the cloth napkin while approaching Ingrid's room. He knocked on the door and moved to the side. She opened the door and then her mouth fell open.

He knew that if he spoke to her, she could easily convince him to let her go, so rather than make it more difficult than it already was, he plunged the steak knife deep into her abdomen, penetrating flesh and organs, repeatedly.

Ingrid gazed into his eyes as blood dripped from her mouth. He continued stabbing her until the life left her body, then he pushed her twitching corpse into the room and closed the door.

She was standing just inside the room when Alex was stabbing her, so he knew the camera down the hall couldn't see what just happened, and when he made his way to the stairs, he kept his head down so the camera couldn't see his face. His heart was broken, but he remained professional.

Once he was back outside in the dry Israeli heat, the first thing he noticed, once again, was the palm trees.

Alex' mind returned to the present when he felt his empty stomach growling. There was food in the refrigerator, but nothing prepared, and Alex didn't want to cook at that time, so he checked his phone for a delivery place in the area and ordered Chinese food, which was something he didn't usually do.

When the food arrived, he devoured it even though he didn't like it much. He told himself he wouldn't order from there again.

After another shot of vodka and a cigar, Alex admired the oil paintings on the wall that featured landscapes from around the world and wondered whose job it was to shop for those things.

He wouldn't even admit it to himself, but he was ashamed. Ashamed that he had the relic in his hand and he lost it. Alex was just thankful that his superiors had let him stay on the case.

After one last shot of vodka, he closed his eyes and thought about his plan for tomorrow morning. He wouldn't be beaten again.

CHAPTER 32

While standing next to Gracie in the back room of the veterinarian's office, thinking about his father tied up and bloody, Danny wiped the tears from his face.

Gracie said, "You should call the police."

"So they can turn me over to the psychopaths at the CIA? No thank you. I have to try and make the trade for my dad again."

"I can't believe this is happening. We better get out of here. You can get one of those prepaid phones on the way to my place."

Danny said, "It's probably not a good idea for me to go to your place."

Gracie hesitated for a moment, then she took a set of keys from her purse. "My boss and his wife are on vacation. Meet me by my car and I'll close up."

Danny headed back out of the veterinarian's office and into the parking lot.

The night air was cool and crisp.

He stood next to Gracie's light blue Camry with his hood over his head, trying to stay out of the light emanating from the streetlamp above while scanning the area for his enemies. Every car that passed and every person who walked by made Danny nervous. He watched the office while at the same time checking the parking lot.

Gracie turned off the office lights then closed and locked the door before heading out of the clinic and into the parking lot where she stepped into her car without acknowledging Danny.

When she turned the key, the radio was blasting top 40 music, which Danny called teeny-bopper music, even though he knew how much she hated when he called it that. She quickly turned it down.

Danny heard the lock click open. He took another quick look around, then jumped into the car.

Gracie started the engine and pulled out into the street

while Danny kept his eyes on their surroundings.

They took the freeway to a neighborhood near the beach that consisted of bright-colored two-story houses, most with red Spanish tile roofs, and all of them with manicured shrubs and flower gardens.

Gracie parked in a large supermarket parking lot. Just as she was about to get out of the car, Danny retrieved the stack of cash he'd taken from the motel and counted it.

"Where did you get that money?"

"You don't want to know." There were five one hundred dollar bills and twenty-five twenties. He handed her a hundred and said, "Get some snacks, too . . . please."

Gracie examined his face for a moment, then she took the money and got out of the car.

She headed into the pharmacy next to the supermarket while Danny waited. She returned in a few minutes with a prepaid phone, two bottles of water, and some chocolate covered peanuts.

After driving another few blocks, they pulled into the driveway of a two-story gray and white house on the corner that featured white columns and a Koi pond in the center of a flower garden.

Gracie turned off her car and then took a deep breath.

Danny exclaimed, "Your boss lives here? I didn't know the vet business was so good."

She didn't respond to his comment, instead, she said, "There's a light on a sensor and a camera pointing at the front door. He didn't tell me I can't have guests, but . . . you know."

"What do you want me to do?"

"Wait in the car until I go inside and disable the alarm and the outside light. Hopefully, it will be too dark for the camera to pick up on you."

"Do you think he'd be watching?"

"He doesn't usually . . . but he might, now that he's away. You never know. I'll just ask him to trust me if he finds out I brought you here."

Danny had plenty of comments to make about him trusting her, however, he didn't want to start a fight, so he kept his comments to himself and said, "Thank you for helping me."

She didn't answer. She just stepped out of the car and approached the front door. The outside light turned on. She opened the door and hurried into the house. A moment later, the outside light turned off.

Gracie stood just inside the front door, waving for Danny to come in.

He got out of the car and hurried into the house without even checking to be sure they weren't followed.

Once inside, Gracie locked the door.

Danny peeked out the front window. When he was satisfied no one was there, he closed the drapes and said, "You can turn on the lights now."

Gracie turned on the lights and then glanced down at a stack of mail on the table next to the door. "I forgot to get the mail. That's why he gave me the keys in the first place."

"Don't go back out there now." Danny admired the high ceilings, bay windows, and polished wood floors while Gracie turned the alarm back on. The furniture was modern and the TV was huge. "Where's their dog?"

"They took her on vacation with them."

The first thing Danny did was open the package and charge the new prepaid phone. "As soon as there's enough charge, I'm going to call my grandpa and see if he's okay."

"Didn't you say they were watching him, too?"

"I'll be calling the hospital phone. I have to know."

"I'm going to the bathroom. Relax . . . you can watch TV . . . but don't move anything. You know my boss has some serious OCD."

"Can I eat something?"

"The refrigerator is pretty much empty. There may be some things in the cabinet. Eat what you want, but don't leave a mess."

Usually, Danny would have responded with a sarcastic

comment. Not this time.

Inside the spacious kitchen with shiny black appliances, all with digital displays, Danny found a few cans of ginger ale in the refrigerator and some sliced bread in the breadbox. After searching through the cabinets, he came up with some peanut butter as well as some potato chips. He made a sandwich then scarfed it down while standing over the island in the center of the kitchen.

Gracie entered. "There's canned foods, too. Soups . . . and some vegetables I believe."

They both ate soup, then Danny checked the charge on the new phone. There was enough to make a call. He first used Gracie's tablet to google the phone number for the hospital, then he used the prepaid phone to make the call. He remembered grandpa's room number, so he typed it in when prompted. The phone rang about eight times and then switched over to a recorded message telling him to try again later.

Danny wondered if grandpa was asleep, or getting something done. He also worried that one of his enemies could have kidnapped him, too.

After plugging the phone back in to charge, Danny said, "I could really use a shower . . . and I was considering shaving off my beard so Victoria or Tsomo won't recognize me as easily."

Gracie had always wanted him to shave his beard. She said it made him look scruffy. She wanted him to get a clean cut hairstyle, too, but Danny liked his scruffy style, and he didn't want to have to shave every single day. He didn't even usually waste time brushing his hair.

"Good idea." She opened a few kitchen drawers until finding some scissors. "We can use these. Check the bathroom for my boss' shaving stuff."

Inside the spacious beige granite bathroom, she used the scissors to cut Danny's hair and beard and then Danny shaved his own face with the razor, leaving behind a couple of small slices. When he washed off the shaving cream and glimpsed at himself in the mirror, he was a different person. His bare face felt numb and he only had a couple of inches of hair left on his head.

"Wow. You are so handsome without all that hair on your face."

Danny said, "Try to control yourself. I don't put out on the first date."

She chuckled and playfully punched him in the shoulder. She took the scissors from him and said, "Let me try to straighten this out." She made the hair on his head even shorter, but it was beginning to become something. Her time as a dog groomer had paid off.

By the time everything was evened out, there was less than a half-inch of hair left on his head. Danny looked like he was ready to enlist. "Imagine what my dad will say when he sees me with this haircut." When he considered the possibility that he may never see his father alive again, his eyes filled with tears that began to run down his face.

Gracie wrapped her arms around him.

When he finally stopped crying, he kissed her.

She kissed him back, just for a moment . . . then she pulled away and said, "We can't do this." She left the bathroom and closed the door behind her.

Danny got into the shower and while he washed, he kept hoping Gracie would come back into the bathroom and join him in the shower, just like she used to do—but she didn't.

The small cuts on his face were bleeding so he stopped the flow with tiny pieces of tissue.

After drying off, he didn't want to put the same dirty clothes back on, so he wrapped the towel around himself and then stepped out into the hall and yelled, "Gracie. Can I wear some of your boss' clothes? Mine need to be washed."

The veterinarian was a bit taller and huskier than Danny was, but wearing loose clothes would be better than putting on the clothes he'd been sweating in all day, especially his underwear. He didn't tell Gracie that he hadn't showered that morning because he woke up late and didn't want to keep his dad waiting.

She called out, "Come see this!"

With just the towel wrapped around his naked body, Danny entered the living room where Gracie was sitting on a leather chair watching the news.

"There was an explosion at your mobile home park."

Danny first thought they had bombed his place, but while he watched, the news showed that it was his friend's house across the street that had exploded. "Skywolf."

"That's your friend's house?"

Danny gulped, then nodded. "Those bastards."

The newscaster said the explosion was caused by a gas leak and that two bodies were found.

"I hope they didn't get to grandpa, too." Danny unplugged the new phone, which had more than twenty-five percent charge. He redialed the number at the hospital and it just kept ringing. "I have to keep trying."

"I'm going to take a quick shower." Gracie headed into the bathroom while Danny settled down onto the sofa and dialed the number again. He called a couple more times but it continued to ring.

Finally, as Gracie was on her way out of the bathroom with wet hair and a robe on, a woman answered the hospital phone. Danny stammered, "Oh . . . um . . . hi. Is this room 289?"

"Yes, it is." Replied the woman on the phone.

"Um . . . I was trying to reach Bob Ackerman."

She said, "Hold on a minute."

Gracie sat down next to Danny.

He inhaled the scent of her freshly washed hair while waiting on the phone.

A different woman got on the phone and asked, "Who is calling please?"

"This is his . . ." Danny was about to say grandson, but he didn't know who he was talking to so he lied, "I'm his son. Is this his room?"

"I'm sorry, sir. We have been trying to reach you. Your father passed on a couple of hours ago."

He didn't even hear what else the woman on the phone was saying. He hung up while she was still talking and repeated it out loud to himself, "Grandpa's dead."

"I'm so sorry." Gracie wrapped her arm around him. "Do you think it was them?"

"I don't know." Danny broke down. He couldn't hold back the tears.

Gracie held him closer.

They held each other for a while, then . . . she kissed him. Her lips were soft and moist and her tongue was tantalizingly delicious. They kissed for a few minutes, then Danny felt his towel slipping off. When he lowered his gaze, Gracie was sliding her hand down between his legs, making his soldier stand at attention. He slipped his hand into her robe and fondled her nipples, which were already erect.

After a quick and passionate round of savage animal sex on the sofa, they lay there kissing and caressing each other's naked bodies for a few minutes without saying anything.

Once again, Danny's soldier rose to the occasion. But that time they took it into the bedroom.

Gracie removed the fancy comforter from the bed and then lay down.

Then, they took it slow and made love.

CHAPTER 33

While Detective Robertson made love to his wife that night, he fantasized about Victoria. He didn't mean to. It just happened. The more he tried to push her out of his mind, the more he thought about her. Her commanding hips that flowed into a tight midsection and her luscious red lips.

It wasn't just her beauty that had him going, it was her tough attitude. She was like a horse that needed to be broken. He felt guilty, but he told himself it was only natural, and then he continued fantasizing about Victoria while satisfying his own horny wife.

After they finished, they cuddled for a moment, then his wife said, "I'm going to check on the boys." She kissed him on the chest and then left the bedroom.

Robertson stared at the ceiling while pondering his case. He had a feeling he was in too deep, but he didn't want to admit it to anyone, especially his wife, who thought of him as a superhero.

He was worried that if he asked for help that he'd be giving up. Not yet.

When his wife returned, she snuggled up next to him on the bed and asked, "What's on your mind?"

"Just mulling over my new case."

"You wanna tell me about it?"

"I would, but I can't."

"Well . . . whatever it is . . . the bad guys better watch out now that my captain America is on the scene."

Robertson chuckled, then kissed her, then closed his eyes and drifted to sleep.

CHAPTER 34

Danny woke up to dreams of violence. Almost jumping off the unfamiliar bed he was lying on. Sweating. Heart pounding. The memory of being choked and almost losing consciousness was burned into his mind, as well as the blast of Victoria's gun when she fired two bullets into that Russian's skull, and the deafening echo that lingered in his ears afterward.

Next to him, Gracie rolled over, but she was still asleep.

He got up without waking her, used the bathroom, then returned to the bed.

After kissing her lightly on the forehead, he lay down and closed his eyes. Danny thought about his grandpa and hoped he died without feeling any pain, and he hoped he died of natural causes.

Grandpa had always been a beacon of hope for Danny and his older sister. He always told them to follow their hearts and do whatever makes them happy.

When Danny said he didn't want to join the army, unlike Dad, Grandpa was sympathetic. However, Grandpa wasn't happy about the way Danny had handled it.

Twelve years ago, when Danny's older sister graduated high school and told everyone she was gay, Dad kicked her out of the house. It was Grandpa who had taken her in and tried to convince their dad to accept it and be happy for her. But of course, their dad was too stubborn. The two of them haven't spoken since then. Now Danny's sister lived with her wife somewhere in northern California and called Danny and Grandpa on holidays.

Grandpa even tried to keep Danny's parents together after his mother admitted that she was in love with another man. She said Dad was too controlling and she couldn't live her entire life like she was in the military.

Danny cried when he realized he would never see his grandfather again, except maybe one day in heaven.

Gracie woke up and put her arm around him. She didn't

have to say anything. Her presence was comforting enough. He kissed her on the cheek and inhaled her scent.

Once again, they fell into a deep sleep, but it didn't last long. Danny woke up again to violent dreams. This time he was screaming and he leapt off the bed.

Gracie jumped up and rubbed her eyes.

Danny said, "Sorry."

"Don't be." She stood, kissed him on the forehead, then entered the bathroom.

Danny went into the kitchen for some water, then retrieved the little leather book from the living room and brought it into the bedroom where Gracie was waiting for him in the bed. She was naked, and she was so alluring, however, Danny had already fired two shots and didn't feel he was ready for another. He pretended not to notice her delicious nakedness and sat down on the bed next to her.

Gracie asked, "What's with the book?"

"I don't know." He flipped through the pages. "It's all in German." He flipped to the back pages where it showed a diagram of the relic with strange symbols on it. "Here's a drawing of it. But it doesn't have those markings on it."

Gracie stood and took her tablet out of her bag. "Let's take pictures of it and translate it."

"Those things don't give perfect translations."

"Does it have to be perfect?"

"I guess not." He flipped back to the first page and then laid the open book on the bed. The pages were yellowed around the edges and brittle. Danny took extra care not to damage it. "This thing should probably be in a museum." He held the pages open while trying to keep his fingertips out of the picture.

She snapped a photo with her tablet and then checked it. "It's too dark. Come over here where there's more light."

Danny moved the book from the bed to the night table, directly under the lamp, and held the pages open while Gracie took another picture. She checked it and showed Danny. He nodded.

Gracie tapped on the screen. "Okay, let's open the translator." She held the tablet over each page while it translated German to English and then she saved each page as a separate document.

After they were finally finished, Gracie returned to the bed and yawned. She must have been reading his mind when she said, "All this time and you haven't smoked any weed."

"You got any?"

He sat on the bed next to her and she playfully punched him in the shoulder.

One by one, they read each translated page on the tablet and filled in the blanks with whatever seemed logical at the points where the translation didn't make sense. Gracie was right. It didn't have to be perfect to get an idea of what the book said.

The book was a journal, written by an SS captain who was in charge of security at an excavation site in the Tibetan mountains.

The first page explained that in 1942, the Ministry of Ancestry decoded a newly discovered ancient text that revealed the location of a powerful, magical, ancient Aryan weapon.

The journal entries began with the SS captain and three young soldiers being assigned to four scientists.

Gracie curled up next to him and listened while Danny read out loud, "Okay . . . let's see . . . the captain's journal."

April 21, 1943: Today we set out by boat from Sicily on our way to the Suez Canal. I hate boats, but an SS Sonderkommando can show no weakness.

April 23: Today was the first day that I did not vomit. I am becoming accustomed to the movements of the sea.

May 1: Finally making our way around the Arabian Peninsula, we took down our German flag and put up a British Flag. Due to British control of India, we will now have to travel disguised as Englishmen. Thankfully, all four scientists in our group speak English, because none of my men understands even a word.

May 12: Finally, land. Thank the gods.

May 13: After only a one day break, we are back in another boat, this one much smaller. We begin our journey upriver at the eastern end of India. Crocodiles are everywhere in the delta and I can hear the squawks, clicks, and chirps of other animals all around me. Sounds I've never heard before. The trees here grow at an angle, creating a roof over the river. The sun is on its way down now, but the heat and humidity don't seem to be letting up.

May 14: Nothing has changed since yesterday. I'm writing this entry because I just encountered a Bengal Tiger. An enormous male. He was strolling toward the river and when he saw our boat cruising upstream, he stopped and looked directly at us. I gazed into his eyes and I could feel his animal existence.

May 19: Once again, land. We reached Sikkim this morning and had to bribe a local guide and an interpreter an absurd amount of money to agree to go with us to Tibet. Another team of German scientists came this way just before the war and ran into a bit of trouble. Now, with the war on, we have to stay far away from the English and the public eye. The last expedition had returned with plant and animal specimens, and a treasure trove of knowledge. But on this mission, there is only one goal. Hopefully, the ministry is right and this ancient technology we are searching for will help the Reich conquer the entire world and ensure Aryan dominance.

May 22: My ass hurts. No one told us we would be traveling up these huge mountains on the backs of donkeys. The air is getting colder and thinner the higher we get.

May 25: We have finally reached our destination . . . that's what the scientists are telling me . . . although I'm not seeing anything except mountains. I hope they know what they're doing. I am fully prepared to give my life for the Reich, but I'd rather die in battle than to die from freezing or starving.

May 26: They were right. We are now at the mouth of a cave that has been sealed off with hundreds of heavy stones, obviously done on purpose, and with care. My men are setting the dynamite. History is about to be written.

Danny heard Gracie snoring. But he wasn't ready to sleep yet. He wanted to know more, so he swiped to the next page on the tablet and kept reading. This time silently.

May 28, 1943: Finally, after removing enough debris for a man to get through, the scientists climbed into the cave with their equipment. They ordered myself and my men to stay outside.

June 2: An old monk in a red robe with an orange sash shows up every day to warn us of the curse surrounding the secret of the mountain. Our translator tells him to go away, but he always returns. He doesn't understand that Germans don't believe in curses. The locals even tried making strange noises with some kind of musical instrument. It was laughable actually.

June 11: The locals have been setting obvious traps that my men have discovered and disarmed. I'd like to set an example by killing a few of their young men and impaling them for others to see, but the scientists, who technically outrank me, have ordered me and my men to refrain from typical SS tactics. If only they understood how effective our tactics could be.

June 20: There was an explosion last night. The locals stole some of our dynamite and used it to cause an avalanche, which sealed off the cave. Against my advice, three of the scientists slept in there every night. Now that cave is their tomb. Except Captain Ulrich, the only scientist smart enough to head my recommendations. He is with us now and it is my duty to protect him.

June 21: I had planned on reopening the cave, but when we returned this morning, we were met with a dozen Tibetans armed with Bergmann submachine guns. They were wearing red robes instead of uniforms, but that didn't matter. They were trying to kill us. My men stayed behind to hold them back while I got Captain Ulrich to safety. Now the sun is on its way down and I haven't heard from any of my men. I believe they are all dead.

June 23: There has been no word from my men. I don't want to leave them, but Captain Ulrich is ordering me to. While we hold the same rank, he is technically my superior. I hereby state that leaving my men, dead or alive, is not my choice. I haven't seen or heard from our interpreter so I must assume that he deserted us.

June 25: As we trek through the mountains, an ancient castle that appears to be carved out of the same mountain it sits upon looms over our heads. I can imagine the Aryan gods that must have inhabited that great structure in the distant past.

June 30: Captain Ulrich is dying. The air here is thin. We are trying to keep warm without a fire. It rains every night and even though it is spring, it is much colder here than in Germany. I just hope it's too cold for any wild animals to be out hunting. He didn't tell me what they found in that cave, but he showed me what he had taken from there. Half of a small black sphere. I don't recognize the material. It may be some kind of stone, or possibly metal. He made me promise to guard it with my life and get it back to Germany.

July 3: Captain Ulrich is dead. I don't have the time nor the energy to bury him, so I must leave him. Forgive me, Captain Ulrich.

July 5: Finally out of the mountains. I ran out of food and water a couple of days ago. The water from the river gives me diarrhea, but it's the only water available.

July 7: Once again, the Aryan gods have guided me. I am in a village and the people here are generous and helpful. My belly is full again. They will bring me down the river tomorrow morning . . . at least that's what I believe they are trying to say.

July 9: Finally, out of the wilderness, I just traded my gun and my watch for safe passage on a cargo ship going to Turkey.

Danny's eyes started to close from all that reading.

He powered off the tablet and set it on the nightstand.

It felt good lying next to Gracie. He put his arm around her and got closer, inhaling her scent and savoring the moment.

And while he tried to fall asleep, all he could think about was Skywolf and Grandpa. He just hoped his dad wouldn't be joining them in the afterlife.

CHAPTER 35

Detective Robertson jumped out of bed when he heard someone pounding on his front door. He grabbed his gun from the nightstand and switched off the safety while whoever was at the door kept pounding.

His wife asked, "What's going on?"

"Go to the boys' room and stay there."

"Baby, you're scaring me. What's going on?"

"Just do it." He stood outside of his bedroom door while his frantic wife hurried down the hall and into their sons' bedroom.

He then marched to the front door and opened it. "What the fuck?" He pointed his gun at the white man and black woman who were standing on his front porch.

With their hands above their heads, the woman said, "Put the gun down, Detective. We are federal agents."

Robertson believed them, but he wasn't going to trust a hunch. He had to be sure. "I'll put the gun down after I see your ID." Robertson turned to the man, and while he knew it was sexist, he assumed the man would be a faster draw than the woman. He pointed his gun at him and demanded, "You first. Let's see it. Slowly."

With one hand, the man reached into his suit jacket.

Robertson wasn't usually paranoid, but people didn't usually bang on his door in the middle of the night. His hand was steady, even though his heart was racing.

Finally, the man showed his CIA credentials. Agent John Wax.

Robertson lowered his gun. "You scared the shit out of my wife. You're lucky I didn't just shoot you both. Why are you here?"

The female showed her ID. "I am Agent Gail Moreau. We need to speak with you about Victoria Becker."

"In the middle of the night? Wait here. I'm going to tell my wife we're not being invaded by terrorists." Robertson didn't invite them in.

He left them standing outside when he went into the house and then into his kids' room where his wife was holding both of their sons, sitting on one of two race car beds, all three of them terrified. "It's okay, baby. It's the CIA. They're here to talk to me about my case."

"My god . . . they almost gave me a heart attack. Haven't they ever heard of telephones?"

Robertson left his wife there and marched back through the living room.

He still didn't invite them in. He stepped outside the house and closed the front door. "What's so important that it couldn't wait until morning?"

Agent Wax said, "We understand Agent Victoria Becker came to see you at the station."

"Yes. I have a case with a John Doe who was found with a couple of bullets in his head and no one knows where the owner of the house is. She wanted his son's arrest records . . . and she wanted the records of the friends he had been arrested with in the past."

Agent Wax said, "Daniel Ackerman."

Robertson got cranky when he didn't get enough sleep. "If you already know . . . then why are you banging on my fucking door in the middle of the night? Scaring my wife and children? Is this how you get your kicks?"

Agent Moreau explained, "This is a matter of national security, Detective. It is not to be taken lightly. We need to know what you and Agent Becker spoke about."

"I'm not taking anything lightly. I'm just saying a phone call would have been nice. You know?" He shook his head. "Anyway, Victoria Becker came to the police station and had me pull up Danny Ackerman's arrest records. And she wanted to know who he'd been arrested with . . . and their addresses, too. I just told you that."

The two agents glanced at each other.

Robertson asked, "I guess the information is only going one way on this?"

Agent Moreau responded, "Victoria Becker is officially

on vacation. It is obvious now that she has gone rogue. We can't tell you more than that. But we will be expecting your full cooperation. Your superiors already assured us you will be happy to help."

Robertson grinned. "Happy? I'm ecstatic. Can't you tell?"

Agent Wax said, "Get some sleep, Detective. We'll be seeing you soon."

He slammed the door in their faces.

CHAPTER 36

Of course, they could have easily called Detective Robertson rather than wake up his entire family in the middle of the night, but then Agent Gail Moreau wouldn't have been able to catch him off guard and look him in the eyes. She wanted to be sure he wasn't helping Victoria.

And it also gave her the opportunity to leave a listening device, which she planted when Robertson went to calm down his wife and kids. He hadn't invited them in, but he'd left the door open, and that's when she planted the bug under a reading lamp sitting on a table next to the sofa.

Now, while sitting in their government-issued gray sedan, Agent Moreau and Agent Wax listened to what was going on in Robertson's house.

They heard Robertson and his wife talking, but they were too far from the bug to provide any usable audio.

The talking stopped, and then, after twenty minutes of not hearing anything, Agent Moreau assumed that Robertson and his wife had gone back to sleep.

Agent Wax yawned.

The yawn was contagious. Agent Moreau yawned too, wishing she had another cup of coffee and wondering how long they should stay there.

Born and raised in a New Orleans ghetto, Agent Moreau spoke impeccable French and Arabic. She had learned French as a child from her grandmother and then perfected it in high school. Coming from a poor family, the only way she could go to college was by joining the military.

She had spent twenty-three years in the US Army where she learned Arabic and worked as a translator. She spent a full year with UN peacekeeping forces in Rwanda during the civil war, and while she was in top physical condition and she was a qualified marksman, she had never been in a combat situation.

When Agent Moreau had retired from the army, she was bored, and still full of vigor, so she applied to the CIA, and they took her right away.

Agent Wax was opening a pack of gum when he stopped and whispered, "I think I heard something."

They listened quietly to things moving around in Robertson's house, and then, the toilet flushed.

Agents Moreau and Wax had originally been assigned to a Tibetan monk who had entered the country with a diplomatic passport yesterday. The monk had slipped past them in the airport. When the Chinese government finally got back to their superiors, they said the monk must have obtained his passport and diplomatic status illegally. They even tried putting the blame on the triads. The CIA knew better than to trust the Chinese government, but they would never be able to prove anything. All they could do was issue a bulletin to all airports and local law enforcement agencies with a description of the monk.

Agents Moreau and Wax were quickly reassigned when Victoria Becker, who was supposed to be on vacation, used her CIA credentials to obtain information from Detective Robertson at the Sunnydale Police Station. Fortunately, the police captain did his job and logged in her visit.

Now, after meeting Detective Robertson, and listening to every little noise in the man's living room, Agent Moreau said, "I don't believe he's helping her."

"Not knowingly anyway," Replied Agent Wax. "But an attractive woman like her can easily convince a man to do things. Things they wouldn't usually do. Not all men possess a fortitude such as mine."

Agent Moreau chuckled. "Please. That girl would have you on your knees faster than a preacher with a shotgun."

He laughed, "I have no idea what that means . . . but you're probably right."

CHAPTER 37

Professor Wagner woke up and glanced over at Victoria, who was sleeping on the other motel bed, the same way she slept as a child. He got up to urinate, which had become a frequent occurrence throughout the night over the past few years.

After returning to the bed, he thought about his wife who died only a few years ago of a stroke. The doctors blamed her high blood pressure, even though she had been taking medication.

The harder he tried to force himself to sleep, the harder it became. He thought about everything that had happened and he felt ashamed that he couldn't get the relic. His ancestors would be disappointed, especially his grandfather's cousin, Colonel Lange, the SS officer who had risked his life to smuggle it from Turkey all the way to Switzerland in the middle of the war.

During his childhood, Professor Wagner had heard the story at least a hundred times, but no matter how many times he'd heard it, he always begged his grandfather to tell it again.

While lying there, staring at the ceiling, the professor closed his eyes and replayed the story in his head.

In the fall of 1943, the Third Reich's hold on Europe was beginning to weaken and they were quickly losing ground in Russia. North Africa was no longer under Axis control, and earlier that month, Italy had surrendered to American and British forces without much of a fight. The Germans started recruiting women and children to help with the war effort. There had been numerous plots from within the Nazi party to kill Hitler that year, and at the same time, Hitler's health was deteriorating, physically and mentally. And on top of all that, there were rumors that Stalin was ready to make an alliance with the western powers.

When the Ministry of Ancestry received news from the German embassy in Turkey about the failed excavation in Tibet and about the SS captain who had smuggled an important relic out of Asia, they sent one of their most trusted and capable members, Colonel Lange.

Colonel Lange had taken a series of trains from Poland to Turkey to retrieve the relic. It was supposedly the most important discovery of the war.

The SS captain who had brought the relic all the way from Tibet was admitted to a Turkish hospital with an unknown stomach virus that had him vomiting all the time and constricted his breathing. He was given a medal and was promoted to major, but he died soon after.

The German embassy provided Colonel Lange with a tall, strong, young SS sergeant as his companion in case of any trouble. And they ran into trouble right away.

On the train coming from Turkey, the first two cars that followed the engine were packed full of chromite ore, which the Germans had been having a problem getting lately and needed badly. The last train car had comfortable seats as well as food and drink for German officers and soldiers. All the train cars in between had square openings for air and they were full of Jews wearing black and white striped prison clothes. The Jews were packed in so tight they had to stand throughout the entire trip.

As soon as they stepped into the last train car with the other Germans, Colonel Lange poured himself a glass of brandy and lit a cigarette. He noticed the young sergeant watching him. "Don't worry, young man. I'm alert. Anyway . . . isn't that why I have you?"

The rhythm of the train rolling along the tracks was relaxing. A few officers fell asleep.

After only a half hour into their trip, there was an explosion followed by a jerking of the train. Everyone stumbled.

The colonel spilled his drink. "Who's driving this fucking train? One of the Jews?" He began to wipe the liquor from his uniform, but then he was thrown to the floor when the train jerked again and then ground to a halt. It leaned to one side, and then returned to its upright position, landing with a crash and throwing everyone the opposite way.

The sound of machine-gun fire erupted outside.

An old fat officer with gray hair and glasses exclaimed, "Bulgarian resistance fighters! Damn it! I told them this would happen!"

The SS sergeant had his MP-40 submachine gun in his hand and was already on his way off the train.

Colonel Lange removed his Luger from its holster and hurried out of the train with the younger men.

The train's engine was lying on its side, spewing out smoke and heat. The two cars with chromite ore were twisted, partially turned over. The cars that housed the Jews were all still standing, yet they were no longer on the tracks, they were all connected but standing in a zigzag pattern. The last few cars were straight and upright.

With nothing except two sets of train tracks going through a wooded area, there was no cover except for the train itself. The young soldiers ducked down and exchanged gunfire with people who could pass for farmers hiding behind the tipped over train engine ahead.

At one point, Colonel Lange had a perfect shot as one of the resistance fighters made a move toward the train cars holding the Jews. He fired, but his pistol wasn't powerful enough to hit the man that far away.

The young SS sergeant turned and fired his machine gun in that direction too late. The Bulgarian fighter had already taken cover.

Most of the high-ranking officers were hiding in the last train car while the young soldiers took all the risk.

Colonel Lange took control and instructed, "We move forward . . . one man at a time . . . one car at a time. Everyone else provides cover fire. When you get close enough, use your grenades." He assigned a number to each man and then said, "Number one . . . ready . . ." He aimed his pistol in the direction of the Bulgarians and yelled, "Cover fire!" He fired his gun, more as a signal than anything.

The German soldiers opened up with their machine guns as number one sprinted ahead to the next train car and then dove behind it.

Colonel Lange yelled, "Cease fire!"

They ducked down and took cover as the Bulgarians fired back with their machine guns.

Colonel Lange yelled, "Reload!"

The Germans reloaded as Bulgarian bullets pinged and ricocheted off the metal train car they were hiding behind.

When the colonel turned around, an old gray-haired colonel was standing next to him. The man was at least in his upper sixties, but he had his pistol in his hand and he was ready to fight. "Don't you dare tell me to stay back there with those old men."

Colonel Lange smiled. "I wouldn't think of it." He glanced ahead at the resistance fighters and said, "Help me provide cover fire." He turned to the others and yelled, "Number two . . . ready!" He and the old colonel next to him both had their guns pointed in the direction of the Bulgarians. When Colonel Lange knew the Bulgarians were reloading, he yelled, "Fire!"

The first young German to stand up took a bullet in the neck. He fell to the dirt with a stream of blood flowing from the wound. The other Germans opened fire.

Colonel Lange reached down, took the submachine gun from the dead soldier's hand, and then began to kill Bulgarians while yelling, "One, two, and three move forward!"

The three young Germans moved forward to their next train cars as the two colonels and the others kept the Bulgarians pinned down with cover fire.

When the first man was close enough, Colonel Lange yelled, "Number one . . . grenade!"

Number one peeked out from behind the train car he

was using as cover and hurled a grenade into the air.

It landed close enough to scare the Bulgarians out of their cover and left them out in the open for the other Germans to easily pick them off as the grenade exploded.

Colonel Lange raced toward the front of the train and the others followed.

A few of the Bulgarians were still alive, but they were badly wounded.

Just as the young Germans were ready to kill the survivors, Colonel Lange stopped them. "Keep them alive. With just the right amount of persuasion, they will tell you who is helping them and where they hide their weapons and supplies." He turned to the older colonel and said, "I have urgent business in Germany. I trust you have everything under control here."

The old colonel raised his hand to give a *Sieg Heil* salute.

Colonel Lange returned the salute and then took his young escort and headed into the woods on foot, going west. "We need to find a vehicle." With the machine gun strapped to his back, the colonel checked and reloaded his pistol and then exclaimed, "Damn, I left my cigarettes on the train!"

They trekked west all night through the dark woods with only the moonlight and their compass' to guide them. The next day they commandeered a vehicle by gunpoint and drove to the Albanian coast.

The Mediterranean was full of Allied ships, so Colonel Lange and the young sergeant bought and changed into civilian clothes and bought a suitcase where they could hide their machine guns. They then paid a lot of money to get on a freighter to northern Italy. The colonel had plenty of cash, fake passports from four different countries, and he spoke six languages. The young sergeant, however, was just a grunt who only spoke German.

Italy had surrendered and the new Italian government declared war on Germany, however, there were German forces who were dug in deep and still fighting, especially in the north.

When the colonel first approached a few German infantrymen, they were suspicious of him due to the civilian clothes he was wearing, however, when he spoke to their commanding officer and told him who he was, they called Berlin to verify his story and then gave him his new orders.

Since there was now the risk of the English and Americans getting their hands on it, and they still had to worry about the Russians who were closing in from the east, Colonel Lange was instructed to bring the relic to Switzerland and lock it in a safe deposit box then report to Austria with the key.

Professor Wagner didn't even realize he had fallen asleep until he woke up to urinate again. He knew he would have to get his prostate checked after this whole ordeal was over and the relic was back in Aryan hands.

Once again, he lay there staring at the motel room ceiling while trying to fall back asleep. This time he thought about where the relic might be and what he would do if they failed to retrieve it. Suicide would be the honorable thing, but he wouldn't do that to Victoria. Other than him, she was all alone in this world.

CHAPTER 38

Once again, Danny woke up in a cold sweat, dreaming of being choked to death. This time, in his dream, blood dripped from the bullet holes in the Russian man's forehead, and although he was already dead, he was still strangling Danny.

When he woke up yelling, Gracie put her hand on his shoulder and said, "I'm here. It was just another nightmare."

It took a second to remember where he was. "You sure your boss won't come back early for some reason? Maybe he has a hidden camera in here somewhere and he's watching us right now."

"I hope not." Replied Gracie, "Then he'll know what a dirty little girl I can be." She giggled.

Danny glanced out the window. The morning sun was barely visible on the horizon.

Gracie was sitting up in the bed, reading the translated journal pages on her tablet.

Danny asked, "What do you think? You think that stuff is for real?"

"I don't know. That thing you have looks like what he's describing in this journal." She scrolled to the last few pages and stopped at a drawing of the relic that included measurements.

"But, what is it?" Asked Danny.

"I don't know. It never says what it is exactly. They just call it a device."

"You read everything?"

"Of course. You know I'm a fast reader."

Danny took the small black half-sphere out of its box and placed it on the bed in between them.

Gracie followed the pattern from the journal while reading the translation on her tablet. She placed her fingertips on the hemisphere's surface.

It glowed blue and began to hum.

She pulled her hand away.

They both stood up.

The relic changed back to its original black color, but now seven blue symbols appeared. Six around the edge and one in the center.

Danny asked, "What the hell?"

"Those symbols look like cuneiform. But they're not."

"I hope it doesn't explode."

They stood there for a few minutes, staring at the illuminated sphere until finally, the blue symbols disappeared leaving just the smooth black finish again.

When Danny remembered that Grandpa was dead and his dad was in the hands of a Russian killer, his curiosity in the relic was replaced by an overwhelming feeling of urgency. He took it off the bed and returned it to the box. "My dad. I have to go."

"I'm going with you."

"I'm not taking the chance of them getting you, too."

But it didn't matter what Danny said, he knew he couldn't stop her.

Before leaving her boss' house, Gracie gave him some of her boss' clothes. A pair of khaki pants and a polo shirt, both two sizes too big.

With nothing else to wear except her smock from yesterday, Gracie tried on some of her boss' wife's clothes. Gracie usually wore pants and blouses, but the ones in the closet were too tight for her to squeeze into, so she opted for a dress with stretchable fabric. Her thick hips and enormous breasts were bulging out of the material and made Danny get a bulge of his own.

"You should wear dresses more often."

"I look like a prostitute."

Danny grinned while adjusting himself. "If you were . . . I'd give you my whole paycheck."

Gracie chuckled. "You don't even have a job."

Danny said, "I guess you're gonna have to give me a freebie then." He placed his hands on her hips and felt that she wasn't wearing any panties. "Hey. Are you naked under there?"

"Wouldn't you like to know?" She pulled away from him and then smacked her own ass cheek before leaving the room.

His hormones began to rush through his bloodstream. He wished they had time for another round in the bedroom, but his thoughts quickly returned to his dad.

He hurried into the living room and noticed Gracie bringing in the mail from outside. "I better come up with a good excuse to tell my boss. That camera outside is definitely going to record you this time."

Danny went outside first and entered Gracie's car, wondering if his car was still in the mission parking lot and hoping it hadn't been towed.

The clear sky was sunny, yet the morning mist provided a cool atmosphere.

Gracie got in the car and then they took off toward the freeway.

Danny texted Alex to meet him at the Sunnydale Mall.

The mall was still closed when they arrived, but Danny knew there were people in there working. He just hoped the security guards didn't come around asking questions.

CHAPTER 39

Tsomo woke up with a dry mouth and a headache. When he saw the morning sun through the window and Miss Stong asleep in her clothes on the other bed, he knew he'd been tricked. He checked anyway, but Danny and the relic were gone.

He woke his cousin and said, "I underestimated him."

Miss Stong rubbed her head.

Tsomo checked the app on his phone. He had two messages from China. The first message said the relic was at a house near the beach and asked Tsomo to verify if he had moved it. The second message was sent hours later and it said that the relic had moved again and was now at the mall. They were still asking Tsomo to verify if he had moved it.

Embarrassed to admit that he had been outsmarted, Tsomo replied with a text that he was on his way to retrieve the relic, then he told Miss Stong, "It is at the mall."

"Give me a minute." She hurried into the bathroom while Tsomo massaged the back of his neck, trying to get rid of his headache. If he were home, he'd rub a natural topical ointment on his head, however, he didn't want to take any drugs, and he knew that's all they'd have in America, so he decided to suffer while his head pounded.

He took one of two bottles of water left on the desk and downed the entire bottle. He wanted more, but instead, he gave the second bottle to Miss Stong when she came out of the bathroom.

She took a few sips of water, then explained, "I think he gave us marijuana. The edible kind. We'll be fine. I just need a couple of aspirin. I have some in my purse."

CHAPTER 40

When Professor Wagner woke up for the final time, he still felt tired.

Victoria's bed was already made and the bathroom door was closed with the light on inside.

He sat up and checked his phone while waiting for her to finish in the bathroom. He scrolled through his regular emails and then checked the news.

While the professor reviewed the weather report, which was clear and sunny, Victoria came out of the bathroom with wet hair and her phone in her hand.

"He's on the move. He texted the Russian and told him that he had taken the relic from the monk and wants to trade it for his father. He's on his way to the Sunnydale Mall right now." She grabbed her bag.

"Give me a minute." He knew he didn't have time for a shower or a cup of coffee, but he had to pee, and that couldn't wait.

After finishing in the bathroom, the professor grabbed his wallet and car keys and then followed Victoria outside.

The sun was already shining bright as cars and trucks zipped back and forth on the street in front of the motel, almost drowning out the songs of the birds in the trees.

Professor Wagner drove the Tahoe while Victoria sat next to him with her eyes on her phone.

Traffic on the freeway was heavy and they were barely moving.

Victoria said, "No time for me to go back for my rental car now. I'll have to go on foot when we get there . . . if we don't lose him by then with this damn traffic." She retrieved a pistol with a silencer from her bag and handed it to the professor.

He made sure the safety was on before slipping it under his seat.

Professor Wagner was trying to convince himself as much as he was trying to convince Victoria when he said,

"We will get the relic. It is our destiny as a race. The gods are just testing us . . . to be sure we are worthy."

CHAPTER 41

After the two CIA agents had left his front door, Robertson peeked out the window to see that they were sitting in their car across the street and a few doors down. He didn't care. He had nothing to hide. And he just wanted to get some sleep.

He had stopped in the bathroom and then returned to the bedroom, where he lay awake in his bed until the sun came up.

His wife slept with the boys in their room. Although she was obviously tired and shaken, she still woke up and tried her best to act normal while making breakfast.

Before leaving the house, Robertson drank an extra cup of coffee and assured his wife one more time that everything was okay.

Outside, the sun was shining bright and the birds were singing their morning songs.

Robertson drove with his windows open all the way to the Sunnydale Police Station while thinking about Victoria. Was she a double agent? A traitor? He didn't want it to be true, however, he remembered from his years in Sunday school that Satan was once the most beautiful angel in heaven.

After parking his car and entering the police station, Detective Robertson was on his way to pour himself a cup of coffee before going to his desk, but then he noticed the two CIA agents who had gone to his house in the middle of the night. They were sitting with the police captain in his office.

When Robertson tried to sneak by the office, his captain saw him and called him in.

He entered the office and put on a fake smile. "Hello, agents. Long time no see."

The police captain said, "The CIA is taking over your John Doe case."

"Taking over?"

Agent Moreau explained, "We usually don't get involved in domestic matters, however, due to the fact that your case may implicate one of our agents, it is our responsibility to investigate it. And as we said before . . . this is a matter of national security."

At his desk, he gave them his files on the case, but when they asked if he had any copies, he lied and said he didn't. For some reason, he felt like he needed insurance.

CHAPTER 42

While sitting with Gracie in her car in the mall parking lot, Danny kept fidgeting. He knew he couldn't mess up again or the Russians would kill his dad. He just hoped Victoria or Tsomo didn't show up.

The mall had just opened and cars began to fill the parking lot. Most of them employees.

"I'm starved." Danny handed her a twenty-dollar bill. "Can you get something from Dunkin Donuts?"

Gracie examined his face once again. She was accustomed to him being broke. It was one of her complaints when they were dating. She was never cheap, but she always said it would be nice if her boyfriend paid the bill once in a while. And of course, her friends all agreed with her. Finally, he was paying for something. He just wished it was under different circumstances.

Danny stayed in the car while Gracie entered the mall.

After only a few minutes, she returned with two cups of coffee and two bagels with cream cheese. A separate paper bag contained an apple crumb donut. Danny smiled when he saw it.

"I remember how much you loved that donut. Too sweet for me."

He kissed her on the cheek. "You are sweeter than the donut." He kissed her again, then licked the frosting from his fingers. "I wish I could lick this sweet stuff from all over your body."

"Danny." Gracie blushed.

After a while, he was dying to go to the restroom. He didn't want to take a chance of going into the mall and missing Alex, so he stepped out of Gracie's Camry and left the door open while pissing on the tire of the pick-up truck next to them.

After he finished, as soon as he was back in Gracie's car, she handed him a mini bottle of hand sanitizer and said, "I don't know how you guys walk around with those things."

While saturating his hands with sanitizer, Danny replied, "Sorry. Next time I'll leave it at home."

She giggled, then her face changed.

Danny turned to see what she was staring at.

A black Mercedes cruised into the parking lot and then stopped in front of the mall entrance.

Alex stepped out of the Mercedes and scanned the area before going into the mall.

The Mercedes drove away, through the parking lot and around the other side of the mall until it was out of sight.

"That looks like the car they had my dad in last time." Danny stepped out of Gracie's car.

"Be careful." Her eyes were moist as she watched him close the car door.

It wasn't far from their parking spot to the mall entrance, but there was plenty of space for a car to come and run him down or for a sniper on the roof to take him out. Danny gripped the little wooden box, which was in the pocket of the oversized windbreaker he was wearing.

Inside, a security guard strolled along the almost empty walkways while a few old men wandered into Dunkin Donuts and middle-aged women were slowly flocking to the nail salon and the hairdresser next door. Employees were opening stores and preparing for their day.

Alex was standing in front of the directory, his back turned to Danny.

Danny approached and stood next to him, both of them pretending to read the map. "Is my Dad in that Mercedes again?"

"I had a feeling you were watching me out there." Alex turned to Danny. "Nice haircut." He glanced both ways, then said, "Before we talk about your dad . . . let's talk about that monk."

"That dickhead? He only cares about bringing that thing to Tibet. He told me that my father's sacrifice will be rewarded in the next life."

"Sounds like something a monk would say." Alex turned

and said, "Walk with me."

They strolled along the open walkway passing a jewelry store, a clothing store, and a game store. Danny couldn't help glancing at the poster in the window of a new game coming out.

"How can you possibly have gotten the relic away from that monk?"

"I dosed him with some edible cannabis. You should have seen his face. He was like a zombie."

"Very clever," replied Alex. "So . . . do you have it with you?"

"It's close . . . but this time I want my dad first. I didn't get it away from the monk just to get ripped off by you. I only care about one thing . . . my dad."

"Then it should please you to know that I didn't break his arm. I was . . . bluffing . . . as you Americans say. I just wanted to keep you on the right track."

"Oh . . . thank god." Danny exhaled and then asked, "And the picture with the blood and the tooth?"

"That was real. I may be a humanist . . . but I am still a professional."

Danny wished he could kill Alex instead of bargain with him. "Did you kill my friend and his grandmother across the street from my mobile home?"

"No. I did not."

Usually, a Russian spy would be high on Danny's list of people not to trust, yet after what he had just been through, and the dangerous people who were still after him, he realized the Russians weren't the only possible suspect. He couldn't do anything about it now anyway, so he tried to keep his mind on the task at hand. "This time we're going to do things different. I want my dad first. Then you'll get what you want."

They circled the hallway passing an ice cream shop that wasn't open yet and a pet store with cute puppies in the window. They followed that walkway around until they were once again at the front entrance.

Alex demanded, "At the same time. You will get your father and I will get the relic . . . at the same time. How do I know you even have it? I haven't seen it."

"You know I have it. It's right outside." Danny had it in his pocket the entire time and was trying to act cool. "I haven't seen my father yet."

They stopped just inside the mall entrance.

The electric doors opened for them and stayed open.

Alex called someone on his cell and spoke a few words in Russian. He then stepped outside and stood on the sidewalk under the clear sunny sky.

Danny stood next to Alex while the electric doors closed behind them.

The black Mercedes appeared from around the corner and then slowed down in front of them. The back window rolled down revealing Danny's bruised up father.

Danny's stomach twisted while a tear rolled down his face. He hated seeing his dad like that, but he was happy this was finally going to be over.

He stepped to the side so Gracie could see him, then he waved for her to come.

Alex asked, "Is it in that car?"

CHAPTER 43

As more cars arrived in the parking lot and people went into the mall, Alex and Danny stepped to the side so they weren't blocking the doors.

Impressed at how Danny had handled the situation so far, Alex knew better than to underestimate him. He watched as a young woman with reddish-blonde hair in a blue Camry pulled up in front of his black Mercedes and left the engine running.

He motioned to the driver of the Mercedes to let Danny's father out of the car. He did.

When the girl stepped out of her car, Alex thought she was coming to give him the relic, instead, she hurried to Danny's dad and helped him toward her car.

Alex turned to Danny, "Your turn."

As the girl helped Danny's dad into the Camry, Danny handed Alex the little wooden box and said, "I would say it was nice doing business with you . . . but I'd be lying." He started to walk away.

Alex opened the box and gazed at the relic inside.

CHAPTER 44

As Professor Wagner circled the mall parking lot in the Tahoe, he spotted two men standing in front of the mall entrance. One of them was definitely the Russian, and the other one could have been Danny with a haircut and baggy clothes, but he wasn't sure. "Is that the kid?"

Victoria was scanning all the parked cars when she turned to see Danny and Alex in front of the mall entrance. "That's him. And the Russian has our box. Step on it."

The professor stepped on the gas pedal. The engine roared as he sped toward the mall entrance.

Danny turned and looked right at them. He turned and yelled, "Gracie, go! Go now!"

A blue Toyota Camry peeled out and sped away from the mall entrance.

Victoria said, "Let me out. You go after that car."

Professor Wagner skidded to a stop.

Victoria jumped out of the Tahoe.

The professor stepped on the gas pedal and sped toward the Camry, which was already out of the parking lot and merging with traffic on the street.

CHAPTER 45

When the Tahoe dropped off Victoria, Danny moved toward the mall entrance.

Alex sprinted to his Mercedes.

Victoria whipped out her gun and yelled, "Stop! You are under arrest!"

Even though her gun was pointed at Alex, Danny was too terrified to make a move. He stood there next to the open doors with his hands in the air, frozen, just hoping that whoever was driving that Tahoe didn't catch up with Gracie and his dad. At that moment, he was ready to sacrifice his own life for theirs.

Alex said, "You may work for the CIA, but I know you're not working for them now. As a matter of fact, I happen to know they are searching for you at this very moment."

Danny took one step closer to the mall doors, which were still open, and he noticed Victoria glancing at him out of the corner of her eye, like a pitcher trying to catch him stealing base. Danny stopped, his hands still in the air.

CHAPTER 46

Just outside the mall entrance, using his Mercedes as cover, Alex fired at Victoria, but she was already on her way down, diving behind a rectangular concrete flower bed.

Bullets ricocheted off the flower bed, leaving pockmarks and chunks of concrete on the ground.

When the mall security guard came outside and saw what was going on, he fumbled for his gun.

Alex's driver was out of the car and crouched down behind it. He fired at the security guard. Two shots to the torso took him down instantly.

Alex' driver stayed behind the car while exchanging gunfire with Victoria, who was still using the concrete flower bed as cover while getting off a shot whenever she could, most of her bullets hitting the Mercedes.

The dying security guard fired an unexpected shot and killed Alex' driver.

Alex popped another magazine into his gun and then fired the shot that ended the security guard's life.

The sound of sirens getting louder in the distance and the fact that his Mercedes was now full of bullet holes and sitting on flat tires made Alex abandon his escape plan.

Danny sprinted into the mall.

Alex followed him in with his gun in his hand, firing in Victoria's direction.

People inside, who were already hiding behind whatever they could find, screamed and scattered when they saw Alex and his gun.

Just before turning the corner, Alex heard Victoria behind him, yelling for him to stop.

He stopped, just about to spin around and shoot at her, but he was too slow.

She fired first and then took cover behind a closed-up metal kiosk.

Alex felt pressure in his chest. Dizzy. Too weak to squeeze the trigger, he felt pressure on his chest again, and then he lost his balance and fell backward, onto the ground. Disoriented.

While glimpsing down at his bloody suit, Alex remembered Ingrid and the expression of betrayal and pain on her face as he stabbed her over and over. Blood was dripping out of her mouth, yet he kept stabbing her. Even as he thought about that night they had spent in each other's arms, he had continued to stab her.

Now it was his turn to die a bloody death.

With his last breath, Alex whispered, "I love you, Ingrid. Now we will be together forever."

CHAPTER 47

Tsomo had arrived at the mall just in time to see the Tahoe dropping off Victoria.

He parked his beige rental car among the other cars in the parking lot and then raced into the mall after the shooting outside was finished. Tsomo knew Danny was planning to trade the relic to the Russians for his father, but now seeing that the others were also there, he wasn't sure who had it.

After entering the mall behind Victoria, Tsomo stepped into a narrow hallway near the entrance that led to the bathrooms while she was shooting at Alex.

When Alex was down and Victoria was up, ready to move toward him, Tsomo snuck up behind her. With a lightning-fast series of moves that he'd practiced thousands of times since childhood, Tsomo took her gun away and struck her in the face with it, knocking her out instantly.

The sound of sirens blared outside while Tsomo rummaged through Victoria's pockets. She didn't have it.

He then hurried to Alex, who was already dead. He found it. Tsomo opened the box to make sure the relic was there. It was.

Sprinting out of the rear entrance, Tsomo spotted Danny hiding behind a dumpster in the back parking lot. Part of him wanted to punish him for tricking him and taking the relic, yet at the same time, Tsomo was impressed. Not only because Danny had outsmarted him, but also because he had risked his life on more than one occasion to save his father.

Tsomo pretended not to see Danny. He moved away from the door and stood against the wall.

Miss Stong pulled up in a Dodge Minivan and stopped.

The side door slid open.

Just as Tsomo was about to get in the van, he yelled, "Daniel! Come now!"

Danny was obviously surprised and terrified when he

peeked out from his hiding spot to see Tsomo and Miss Stong waiting for him.

He raced toward them and jumped into the van.

CHAPTER 48

When Professor Wagner had tried to get out of the mall parking lot in the Tahoe, he got stuck as a big rig truck passed in front of him and stopped. He beeped his horn, but the bearded truck driver just showed the professor his middle finger while preparing to make a wide turn.

He considered driving to the other side of the parking lot where the entrance to the street wasn't blocked, but he didn't know the area, and he knew he'd lose the Camry.

Finally, the big rig finished making its big turn.

Professor Wagner tore out of the parking lot and then got stuck again, this time at the next intersection when the light turned red. He thought about running through the light, but traffic was heavy, and he knew he'd probably just end up in an accident. Hopefully, the box was with the Russians at the mall and Victoria had it in her hands by now. Hopefully, the Aryan gods really were protecting them.

The light turned green and the professor followed the majority of traffic toward a freeway ramp. If they did get on the freeway, he'd never catch up to them now.

He turned left and decided to circle around and go back to the mall for Victoria.

Just as he was about to make another turn, he spotted the blue Camry coming down the street in front of him. He knew it was the same car when he noticed the girl with the reddish-blonde hair driving. They must have been on their way back to the mall for Danny.

Professor Wagner thanked the Aryan gods, then he stepped on the gas pedal as hard as he could. Rubber burned as the Tahoe took off like a rocket.

His blood was full of adrenaline when he T-boned the Camry, smashing into the driver's side door.

The airbags inflated, saving the professor from smashing his face against the dashboard while at the same time, the Tahoe's hood popped open.

Sparks flew as the Camry spun around twice until finally

smashing into a metal pole. Flames and steam shot out of the engine compartment upon impact.

The professor couldn't see through the windshield with the bent hood sticking up, so he stepped out onto the street.

All the cars in the area had stopped. Many of the people were out of their cars watching.

No one came out of the Camry, but the flames continued to grow bigger and hotter.

Professor Wagner reached for the gun under the seat and was about to approach the car to look for the box when two paramedics jumped out of their ambulance and raced toward the burning Camry. Spectators came from everywhere to gawk at the burning wreckage.

Other than killing the two paramedics and possibly a good Samaritan or two in front of a crowd of witnesses, then searching through a twisted flaming wreck of metal that could possibly explode, the professor had no choice but to flee the scene.

He pushed his bent hood down. It didn't go down all the way, but it was enough for him to see through the windshield. The engine made noise and the car rolled unevenly as it spewed steam from the radiator.

People yelled at the professor to stop as he took off. He tried to tune them out, hoping no one would try to be a hero and attempt to apprehend him. He clipped a couple of other cars while trying to get away.

After only a few blocks, the engine finally blew. A forceful clunking sound was followed by a sudden stop. Professor Wagner grabbed his gun and bolted.

CHAPTER 49

Once again, the senior homicide detective was in court, leaving Detective Robertson on his own.

When he had first gotten the call, he thought there was a surge of violent crimes happening in Sunnydale, but when he heard that two of the corpses were also Russians in fancy suits, he knew it had something to do with Victoria.

With his phone in his hand, Robertson was ready to call Agents Moreau and Wax, but then he decided to wait. Not only in case he was wrong about the Russian connection, but it would give him the chance of doing some real crime solving. They would be there eventually.

When he arrived at the mall, the forensics team was there doing their job, so rather than get in the way, Robertson headed to the security office where the security manager was waiting for him.

Inside the cramped musty office with a wall full of monitors and two desks, each with their own desktop computer, Robertson shook hands with the security manager, a former Los Angeles police officer who had been shot while on duty in a drug bust.

They already knew each other. When Robertson was in uniform, he'd come to the mall a few times to pick up shoplifters who had been caught by mall security guards.

Robertson said, "I'm sorry about your man."

"A damn shame. Good man. He just retired from the Navy last year. I hired him a few months ago. He only wanted to work part-time for some extra spending money. His daughter is pregnant. Damn shame." The security manager tapped a few keys on one of the computers and then moved to the side so Robertson could see. "I don't envy your job today."

"Thanks for the encouragement." Robertson parked himself and stared at the monitor. He thought he was watching an action movie rather than a mall security video.

He watched as Danny Ackerman followed the Russian

into the mall and then a few minutes later, they returned and traded a beaten-up old man for a small square object.

When a black Chevy Tahoe arrived and stopped, Robertson recognized the woman who got out. Victoria.

The Tahoe chased a blue Camry out of the parking lot while at the same time, there was a shootout in front of the mall . . . that's when the security guard and one of the two Russian's was killed. Victoria then chased Danny and the other Russian into the mall.

He checked the videos from other cameras and saw the shootout inside the mall and an Asian man in a sweatshirt and a baseball cap who disarmed and knocked out Victoria before going through her pockets. He then rummaged through the pockets of the dead Russian and obtained a little wooden box.

Another video showed Danny going out to the rear parking lot and then the Asian man going out the same way.

One of the parking lot cameras facing the building provided a view of a Dodge Minivan that picked up the Asian man and Danny. The same camera showed Victoria staggering out the door a few minutes later and then hiding behind an SUV while a patrol car with its sirens flashing entered the mall parking lot.

The patrol car stopped at the rear entrance and a uniformed cop jumped out of it and raced into the mall.

Robertson waited to see where Victoria went, but because of the limited view, there was no video footage of her escape. She could have gone anywhere.

Robertson reversed the video and then stopped it to write down the license plate numbers of the Dodge Minivan and the Chevy Tahoe.

He was just about to call the plate numbers into the police department when his phone rang.

It was Agent Wax.

Robertson told him what he had just seen on video and that Victoria was already gone by the time he'd arrived.

CHAPTER 50

Agent Moreau was sitting next to Agent Wax in her office when he spoke on the phone with Detective Robertson about what had just happened at the mall.

The detective forwarded copies of the surveillance camera video clips.

After ending his call with Robertson, Agent Wax said, "The detective has a clear shot of the minivan's license plate, and the Tahoe, but not the Camry. He's checking into them now. I'll be right back. Nature calls." He stepped out of the office.

Agent Moreau proceeded to log into her computer and searched the federal database for all security cameras installed in the area. There was a post office near the mall. Using the access that only the CIA had, she pulled up a copy of the post office video from that day. There were two cameras inside the post office and one outside. She only downloaded the video from outside and then she fast forwarded until the specified time.

Not long after the Tahoe had followed the Camry out of the parking lot, something happened to make people stop their cars in the middle of the street.

She had a feeling this was a related incident, so she scrolled through the calls made to 911 at that time and found that there had been a hit-and-run involving a blue Camry and a black Tahoe.

The Tahoe was found abandoned and smashed up a few blocks away. The driver of the Camry, Gracie Johnson, was in the hospital and her passenger, Daniel Ackerman, had refused medical treatment and was on his way to the police station to make a statement.

Agent Wax returned with a few freshly printed sheets of computer paper in his hand, "Well . . . I never made it to the restroom, but I did learn something useful. That was definitely the same monk who lost us at the airport yesterday. He seems to be after the same thing as Victoria and the Russians. And it seems we're being given information on a need to know basis."

"Not the first time." Agent Moreau knew that was part of the job. She told Agent Wax what she had just learned about the car crash and then she said, "You go to the police station and find out what Ackerman knows. I'll go to the hospital and make sure none of those lunatics come after that poor girl."

CHAPTER 51

After leaving the smashed Tahoe on the street, Professor Wagner had escaped by running through an apartment complex and then entering a supermarket where he grabbed a shopping cart and rolled it down the aisle while calling Victoria just to find out that she didn't have the relic.

She was on foot, on her way to Daniel Ackerman's neighborhood where she had left her rental car parked the day before. She said, "Stay where you are. I'll pick you up."

Although he knew she was a capable woman, the professor still thought of her as his little girl. "Be careful, *Liebling*." He ended the call and tried not to worry.

He bought a few pieces of fruit and a couple of bottles of water from the supermarket, then headed next door to In-N-Out Burger. Not usually one for fast food, he had eaten at that chain before in Texas and liked it.

A car came out of the drive-thru, then Professor Wagner walked in front of the next car as it pulled up to the pick-up window. There were two empty tables with chairs outside.

Inside, there were no seats, so he ordered his food and ate it outside while hoping no one recognized him from the accident that was less than ten blocks away.

He texted Victoria with his current location while worrying that the driver of every car that passed knew who he was and was calling the police on him. Fortunately, that was only his paranoia. He ate his lunch without incident and then he felt relieved when Victoria pulled into the parking lot in a light gray Chevy Cruze.

Professor Wagner squeezed into the little car. "You weren't kidding when you said you rented something inconspicuous."

"It may not drive like a Tahoe . . . but no one will remember me."

He asked, "Any word?"

"Most likely the monk has it . . . I don't know for sure. But one thing I was able to find out . . . the girl who was driving that Camry was taken to the hospital."

"And the kid?"

"No idea. But I have a hunch he'll be going to the hospital."

CHAPTER 52

Detective Robertson left the mall and hurried to the police station where he found Daniel Ackerman, Sr. sitting on a chair in the break room with his eyes closed and a cup of coffee on the table next to him.

He was just about to wake him up when a uniformed cop entered with a folder and said, "I was going to leave this on your desk."

Robertson glanced over to see that Daniel, Sr. still hadn't opened his eyes. He motioned with his head for the uniformed cop to follow him out into the hall where he took the folder and thanked the officer.

He flipped through the pages before going back into the break room where he poured himself a cup of coffee and settled down on the sofa across from Daniel, Sr.

The detective sipped his coffee while thoroughly reviewing the documents he had just received.

Daniel Ackerman, Sr. began to snore, then stopped and opened his eyes. He stared at Detective Robertson.

Robertson said, "A lot of people have been looking for you."

"Who are you?"

"I'm Detective Robertson. Do you know what happened?"

"I was kidnapped. Those commies wanted the box my father had. Is Danny okay?"

"He's fine. Or so it seems by watching the video. We can't know for sure unless we find him. Do you know where he might go?"

"He'd go to Gracie. In the hospital. Do you know what happened with her? Is she going to be alright?"

"The doctors are hopeful." Detective Robertson continued, "Your son's car was towed from the Mission at San Juan Capistrano a couple of hours ago. It seems that he left it parked there overnight. It's in impound now. There was also an incident there with a man who had been attacked coming out of the basilica. Would you know anything about that?"

"How could I? I was tied up and smacked around. Now you want me to do your job for you?"

Agent Wax entered the break room and showed his CIA credentials. "I know you've been through an ordeal, Major, however, I do need to ask you some questions." He turned to Detective Robertson and asked, "Can you set us up with an interview room?"

CHAPTER 53

Agent Moreau used her CIA credentials and the excuse of national security to illegally review Gracie's chart at the hospital.

Gracie suffered from bruising to the brain, which had kept her in a coma, however, the doctors said they believe that when the swelling goes down, her brain functions would return to normal. There was no evidence of internal bleeding, but she did suffer from a broken arm and leg on her left side where the impact occurred.

After reviewing the chart, Agent Moreau stepped into Gracie's room. She stared at the young comatose girl as machines pumped oxygen into her lungs and kept her heart rate monitored.

When Agent Moreau's phone vibrated, she stepped out of the room and found a text message from Agent Wax telling her that he was at the police station and was about to question Daniel Ackerman Senior. She texted him back telling him she would stay at the hospital in case anyone showed up there.

At the end of the hallway, Agent Moreau bought a can of ginger ale and some peanuts from a vending machine before sitting down on one of the chairs in a waiting area. She had a clear view if anyone entered Gracie's room.

Her phone vibrated again. It was another text message. But that time it was from her ex-boyfriend, apologizing for the thousandth time for cheating on her. She deleted the message, and then she finally blocked his number. She didn't intend to forgive him and she didn't need any distractions.

CHAPTER 54

Danny wanted to find out what had happened to Gracie and his dad, but he had no choice but to escape with Tsomo and Miss Stong in her minivan.

She drove to a motel many miles away from the one they had stayed at previously.

All the way there, Danny used his prepaid phone to call Gracie's cell. When she didn't answer, he left a voicemail for her to call him back. He called a few more times and then left a text message. He even tried calling her house phone a few times and left messages. He tried but failed to hold back his tears when he thought about the possibility of Gracie and his dad being captured, or worse.

Tsomo glanced at Danny as they got out of the minivan in the motel parking lot.

Danny wiped his tears and snapped, "What?"

Tsomo didn't answer, he just followed Miss Stong up the metal staircase to the second floor, and then into a room that looked the same as the last motel room.

"Now you have your toy. What about my dad and Gracie?"

Tsomo entered the bathroom and closed the door.

Miss Stong sat on one of the two beds and said, "I will try my best to help you. Hopefully, they got away."

"And what about your cousin? Is he gonna help me?"

She shook her head. "His life has one purpose . . . and that is to protect the secret of the mountain."

"Now you sound just like him. I can't believe my fifth-grade teacher is a spy."

"I am not a spy. I am a protector."

Danny handed her the stack of cash. "Sorry I took your money. I spent some, but I'll pay you back as soon as I get my check."

"I don't care about that. Keep it. You will need it to get your car out of impound."

After all that had happened, Danny had forgotten about

his car.

Tsomo returned from the bathroom and sat next to Miss Stong.

CHAPTER 55

Tsomo had no intention of risking the relic just to help Danny, however, he did hope that Danny's father and girlfriend were okay.

He said, "I wish I can make you understand how important this is. The secret that we protect is a weapon more dangerous than anything man has ever made. A weapon of the gods."

Danny replied, "Again with the gods. First, it's Nazi technology . . . now, it's a weapon of the gods?"

Tsomo replied, "It is not Nazi technology. It is of the gods. The Germans learned about it from the ancient stories and came to Tibet searching for it. Their first expedition was in 1938, when our grandfather was the chief protector. It was easy to lead them away from the secret that time. But when they returned five years later, it seemed as if they had known exactly where to go. Our grandfather and the others tried to use the same tactics that our people had used for thousands of years, but the Germans didn't believe in curses, and our fake magic did nothing to scare them. Our grandfather was forced to bury them alive in the mountain using their own dynamite. Our people had learned too late that the mind of Krishna had already been removed from the mountain." Tsomo explained, "Since childhood, I have been trained to do two things. To protect the secret of the mountain and to retrieve the mind of Krishna if its location becomes known again."

"That's what you said at the hospital parking lot . . . the mind of Krishna. How is that thing in the box the mind of Krishna?"

Miss Stong added, "A more accurate translation would be brain rather than mind . . . but it's actually more of a key."

"A key? A key to what?"

Tsomo glared at his cousin. She obviously knew what he was thinking when she stopped talking and lowered her head. Tsomo said, "As I told you before, other than the protectors, no mortal man shall possess this knowledge. I am just trying to make you understand how important this is. Upon reaching adulthood, I had to pass a series of difficult and dangerous tests designed to evaluate not only my physical and mental abilities but my morality as well. Not everyone lives through the tests. It wasn't until after passing the tests that I was entrusted with the secret of the mountain." He showed Danny a metal coin hanging around his neck from a leather string. "This is the amulet of the protectors. It is made from the metal of one of Krishna's fallen enemies."

Danny squinted while staring at the coin. "That looks like one of the symbols on the relic."

Miss Stong asked, "You activated it?"

Tsomo warned, "That was not wise."

"Don't tell me that thing is radioactive or something."

Miss Stong assured Danny, "Don't worry. It's not radioactive."

Tsomo said, "Remember . . . I have sworn to give my life to protect the secret . . . and while I will not take a life for any other reason . . . I will kill anyone who tries to take the mind. Including you. Do not try it again."

CHAPTER 56

When Professor Wagner and Victoria arrived at the hospital, they tried their best to stay out of view of the cameras without appearing suspicious.

The first thing they did was sneak through the emergency room and into the busy hallway behind a set of double doors. They followed the polished white floors around the corner, not knowing where they were going, but checking the signs on the walls as they searched for the staff locker rooms

Names of doctors were called out over the loudspeaker system above while hospital staff rushed past them with a patient on a stretcher.

When they finally found the locker rooms, which were a long way from the emergency room where they had entered, the professor was worried about how many cameras had seen them on their way there.

Victoria entered the women's locker room while Professor Wagner entered the men's.

Gray metal lockers took up an entire wall while an open set of shelves on the opposite wall revealed stacks of blue hospital scrubs and long white lab coats, all individually wrapped in clear plastic.

He found his size then quickly slipped a white lab coat over his suit and hoped no one would notice his shiny Italian shoes.

Once he was back out in the sterile white hallway, Professor Wagner found Victoria, also in a white lab coat. He nodded his head and said, "Doctor."

"Did you expect me to go for the scrubs?" She glanced down at his shoes and then at her own black shoes with a short heel and said, "Not exactly physician footwear."

Professor Wagner noticed a young man sitting behind a computer in an office down the hall. "You're up."

Victoria freshened up her lipstick, opened the lab coat and a couple of buttons on her shirt to reveal her cleavage, then she entered the room and tried to get his attention. "Excuse me."

The professor stood outside the door, pretending to text on his phone while watching what was going on inside the office.

The young man answered without looking up. "How can I help you?"

She pushed her breasts up a bit higher, then said, "I am trying to locate a patient. Her name is Gracie Johnson. Can you please find out what room she's in?"

"Are you a family member?" He finally looked up and stared straight at her cleavage. "Oh . . . hello doctor . . . I've never seen *you* here before."

"I'm new. I'm here to do my residency. I don't want anyone to know I got lost on my first day here." She batted her eyelashes then smiled at him like she was ready to sleep with him. "Can you help me?"

"No problem." He glanced back down at his computer but kept glancing back up to ogle her breasts.

Professor Wagner knew she had to behave that way sometimes, although he didn't want to have to see it, so he moved out of view, yet kept listening.

The young man asked, "Are you married?"

"I'm single. Are you married?"

"No. Maybe we can go for a drink or something sometime?"

"Yes. That sounds nice. Is that clock right? Oh . . . I'm going to be so late."

"Don't worry. I found her." Replied the young man. "Gracie Johnson is on the third floor. Room 310."

"Thank you so much. I have to run." On her way out of the room, Victoria motioned with her head for the professor to follow her.

As they hurried down the hall and toward the elevators, Professor Wagner could hear the young man saying, "Wait. What's your name?"

Once inside the elevator, Victoria pressed three and

moved to the side, out of view.

A few more people followed them into the elevator, all of them staring at Victoria's décolletage.

The door opened on the second floor and a few people stepped out, then the elevator continued up to the third floor and the doors opened again.

Professor Wagner and Victoria stepped out into an identical white hallway and then the professor said, "You can button up now."

She turned away from him and buttoned her blouse back up to the top then closed the lab coat.

Professor Wagner scanned the room numbers on the doors as they strolled past them and then he noticed a black woman in a gray pants-suit sitting on one of many chairs at the end of the hall. Not only was she there alone, but the professor could tell by her demeanor that she was some kind of law enforcement or government agent. "See that woman there?"

"Already spotted her." Victoria stepped around the corner, out of the woman's line of sight.

He casually followed her around the corner. "She'll see if either of us go into that room."

Victoria said, "If you can block her view. I can be in and out and back here in a couple of minutes."

Professor Wagner cracked his knuckles and admitted, "This is too much excitement for an old man." He stepped around the corner and strolled toward the woman sitting at the end of the hall. Once he was in front of her, he tried not to move and hoped she couldn't see what was going on behind him.

He spoke to her in German, and once he was sure she didn't understand what he was saying, he began to ramble.

He told her an old bedtime story, and although she tried to interrupt him a few times, he just pretended not to hear her and kept speaking German, all the while trying to block her view.

She finally raised her voice and said, "I'm sorry . . . I

don't speak German."

Professor Wagner stopped speaking and thought of what to say next while wondering if Victoria was in Gracie's room.

The woman asked him in French if he spoke French, and although he did speak French, he pretended he didn't.

The professor then continued in perfect English, "I'm sorry. My colleague's patient has a family member who only speaks German . . . so I offered to translate. I thought it was you."

"It's not me."

"I see." He tried to keep her attention when she moved her head and peered down the hallway. He asked, "Was there another woman sitting here with you?"

"No." She replied. "A man and a boy were here earlier. But it's been quiet for the most part." She moved her entire body to get a better view.

Professor Wagner hoped Victoria had already been in and out of the room. But, he didn't want to take any chances, so he tried to keep the woman in front of him occupied for just a while longer. "You speak beautiful French."

The woman was obviously no longer willing to entertain him when she stood up from her chair and marched right past him, ignoring what he was saying.

She entered Gracie's room.

Professor Wagner was confident that Victoria was already out of there, but he wanted to be sure, so he entered Gracie's room and asked, "Is everything okay?"

The woman was alone. She said, "Everything is fine."

"Okay. Good day then." The professor stepped out of the room and strolled down the hall. When he turned the corner, Victoria wasn't there.

Just as he was about to turn around, he spotted her, on the other side of the elevators.

They took the stairs down to the cafeteria on the first floor where they sat together at an empty table.

Victoria pulled out a phone with a smashed screen. "No box . . . no journal. I just hope the kid has it. If the monk has it, he could be halfway to Tibet by now."

He looked at the smashed phone and asked, "Is it working?"

She snapped the back cover on tight and held down the button. After a few seconds, parts of the screen lit up, but nothing was visible. "It's working. Except . . ." She jiggled the back cover around and tried to snap it down harder. "I can barely see anything."

Professor Wagner surveyed the people who were eating, drinking, or just sitting there, and he didn't feel like any of them seemed suspicious. Yet he was still worried. "Maybe we shouldn't stay here."

"We're better off in here than out there." Victoria squeezed the phone screen in certain places until she was able to see the symbols at the bottom. She then clicked the phone button and a list of phone numbers came up. "I found her call log, but I can't clearly read the names or numbers. This one . . . maybe . . . it looks like the only name that begins with a D." She pressed the screen, then it changed. She held it up to her ear and said, "It's ringing."

Professor Wagner felt a bit of hope returning.

CHAPTER 57

In the motel room, Danny was watching the news while Tsomo prepared his luggage.

Danny jumped off the chair when his phone rang. He checked it and saw Gracie's number. He answered, "Gracie, thank god."

Victoria answered. "Gracie is not well. And there is always the possibility that she may take a turn for the worse and die . . . but that is entirely up to you."

Danny covered the phone with his hand and turned to Tsomo and Miss Stong who were both listening while pretending not to. He whispered, "It's Victoria . . . the rogue CIA agent."

Victoria continued, "Are you with the monk?"

Danny didn't look at Tsomo when he answered, "Yes."

"And does he have the relic?"

"Yes."

"You will retrieve it from him and bring it to me at the hospital. Text me at this number when you are here and I will tell you where to meet me. If you fail to retrieve it or if you try to trick me . . . your girlfriend's oxygen machine will accidentally malfunction. I cannot imagine what death by suffocation must feel like."

"You fucking bitch."

"Save your anger for the retrieval of the box. Your girlfriend's life depends on it."

"I have enough anger for both of you, you fucking bitch . . . you better not touch her. She has nothing to do with this." The screen on Danny's phone lit up. Victoria had already ended the call. He glared at Tsomo and Miss Stong, "She's going to kill Gracie if I don't bring her the box."

Neither of them answered. And that was answer enough.

"This is your fault. I know you won't give it up . . . but you should at least help me get Gracie to safety. She's in the hospital because of you and your stupid relic."

Miss Stong said, "You can't blame us for that."

"I can . . . and I am. If she dies . . . I'll fucking kill both of you!" Danny's rage boiled. He ripped the motel phone out of the wall and threw it at Tsomo.

Tsomo moved to the side in a flash, avoiding the flying phone, then he lunged forward and grabbed both of Danny's arms, twisted them behind his back, and began to squeeze.

Danny tried not to show that he was in pain while Tsomo kept pressure on his arms, almost breaking them.

The more Danny struggled to get out of the hold, the tighter it became.

Miss Stong yelled something in their language.

Tsomo yelled something back and then she yelled again, even louder, and Tsomo finally released his grip.

Danny wanted to hurt Tsomo, but he just wasn't physically capable, not in a fair fight anyway. He would have waited for another chance, but he knew Tsomo wouldn't be that stupid again. Tears filled Danny's eyes while the blood rushed back into his numb arms and hands. "They're going to kill her!"

Miss Stong said, "You have to contact the authorities. The police . . . or the FBI. But we cannot help you. Tsomo must get the relic back to Tibet as soon as possible, and I'm afraid I alone wouldn't be of much help to you."

Tsomo slumped down onto the bed and lowered his head.

Danny began to cry, then he stopped himself. He had an idea. "Can you at least give me the empty box?"

Tsomo lifted his head. "I will give you the empty box. However, I do not recommend you go there alone. You may be walking into a trap."

"You're not gonna help me . . . and I don't have anyone else . . . and I don't trust the cops or even the FBI . . . fuckers . . . not after what I've just been through."

Miss Stong said, "I'm sorry you were dragged into this."

Tsomo had the little wooden box in his hand, and it was already empty. He handed it to Danny and said, "I too am sorry for your suffering, and for the suffering of your family and friends. I wish you well." Tsomo then handed Danny his hunting knife.

Miss Stong warned, "This is not a good idea. Don't forget . . . they have guns."

"I have to try." Danny snapped the battery back into the prepaid phone and connected to the motel Wi-Fi so he could use the internet. He found the phone number for the hospital, then called. He asked for Gracie Johnson. They told him she was there, but she was unable to speak. Danny tried to hold back his tears while asking about his father, who was not there. The woman on the phone must have sensed his desperation and sorrow because she took a few minutes to find out that Danny's father had gone to the police station to make a statement.

After hanging up with the hospital, Danny obtained the number for the police station, and when he called and told them his name, they connected him with Detective Robertson.

CHAPTER 58

Detective Robertson's desk phone rang, and when he answered it, the officer on the line told him that Danny Ackerman Junior was on hold and would like to speak with him. He transferred the call over. "Danny? This is Detective Robertson. Are you in any danger?"

Danny replied, "Not yet. The hospital told me that my father is there . . . at the police station. Is he okay?"

"He's here. And he's fine. But he's busy answering questions at the moment. You should come down here and pick him up. We need you to fill in some of the blanks anyway. And there are still some dangerous people out there. You'd be safer here."

"They're going to kill my girlfriend if I don't give them what they want."

Robertson asked, "What is it they want, Danny?"

"I'm on my way to the hospital right now. I can use some help."

"You need to give me more to work with."

"I'm going and that's it. Help me now or come for my dead body later."

CHAPTER 59

At the hospital, down the hall from Gracie's room, Agent Moreau couldn't sit any longer. Her bladder was full. She stood in the waiting area, checking her phone and wondering if she should take the chance and go to the restroom.

No one knew if anyone would come after Gracie Johnson. Her being there was just a precaution . . . or at least that's what she told herself to justify her notion of leaving her post and going to the restroom.

She played Tetris on her phone while rocking back and forth from foot to foot, trying to convince herself she didn't have to pee when her phone beeped.

It was a message from Agent Wax telling her that he was going to follow a lead on the man in the video who had knocked out Victoria. That message was followed by another message that told her Detective Robertson was on his way to the hospital and should be there any minute.

Detective Robertson entered the hospital and headed for the elevators.

He already knew Gracie's room number, so he waited for the elevator doors to open and then he entered with a few other people.

As soon as he arrived on the third floor, he spotted Agent Moreau down the hall with a painful expression on her face. He approached and asked, "Are you okay?"

"I need to use the restroom."

"I'll be right here."

Agent Moreau scurried down the hall and then disappeared into the women's restroom.

Detective Robertson approached Gracie's room and glanced inside, but he didn't enter. Instead, he strolled to the end of the hall and took a seat next to two women in the waiting area while keeping his eyes on the hallway and waiting for Agent Moreau to return.

Professor Wagner had been hanging around the third floor waiting for Danny while Victoria stood watch on the first floor.

The professor had kept his distance from the woman in the gray suit, but now someone was there to relieve her. Still unsure of whether they were local law enforcement or federal agents, it didn't matter anyway, the end result would be the same if they were captured.

He glanced at his reflection in a window, and other than his shoes, he was satisfied he could pass for a real doctor.

He felt nervous, but it was exhilarating. It was like when Thor and Loki dressed as women to get Thor's hammer back from Thrym, the giant who had stolen it and said he'd return it only for Freya's hand in marriage. Of course, Thor was victorious. He shot lightning bolts from his eyes and then crushed Thrym's skull.

Professor Wagner strolled down the hall.

He paused momentarily when, from an adjoining hallway, Danny Ackerman turned the corner just in front of him, heading toward Gracie's room.

When Detective Robertson spotted Danny Ackerman, he turned his face to the TV hanging on the wall.

Danny didn't seem to pay attention to Robertson or anything else as he entered Gracie's room.

Robertson stood. He didn't see Agent Moreau returning from the restroom yet.

A doctor removed the chart from the wall outside of Gracie's room and then entered.

Robertson noticed how polished his shoes were and wondered if all the doctors dressed like that at work. He then thought about the dead Russians and considered the possibility that that doctor may not be a doctor at all.

Detective Robertson moved slowly toward the room, unbuttoning his suit jacket.

Danny stood in front of Gracie's bed and sobbed while the oxygen machine and the heart monitor beeped rhythmically.

He had always heard that unconscious people could sometimes hear the voices around them, so he moved close to her bed and said, "I'm so sorry. I love you so much. I wish I can trade places with you." Danny wondered if she'd ever wake up, but he didn't say that aloud.

He turned to see a doctor coming in, but on second glance, he realized the doctor wasn't a doctor. It was Professor Wagner, and he knew that meant Victoria couldn't be far.

The professor said, "Once we have the relic, we will leave you and your family alone forever."

Danny reached into his jacket pocket and grasped the little wooden box with his sweaty hand, trying to gauge the weight of it and hoping it felt as heavy with his prepaid phone in there as it did when it contained the real relic. He took a deep breath, then handed him the box.

Professor Wagner grabbed the box and opened it to find a cell phone.

Danny already had the hunting knife in his other hand. He lunged toward the professor.

The professor moved to the side while knocking over Gracie's IV pole. Danny's knife slashed the professor's arm, just enough to make him bleed, yet not enough to stop him.

Danny was ready to lunge again, but when he saw Gracie's IV bag falling to the floor, he was distracted long enough for Professor Wagner to reach into his lab coat and retrieve his gun.

The professor stepped back, racked and pointed his gun at Danny, then said, "Nice try, kid. I have to say, you have impressed me. Now . . . lay that knife down on the bed next to your girlfriend and give me the relic."

Detective Robertson heard a ruckus so he retrieved his pistol from his shoulder holster and hurried into Gracie's room.

The doctor's arm was bleeding and he was holding a gun with a silencer at Danny's head.

Robertson had a clear shot. "Drop it or you're dead!"

"Don't shoot." The doctor lowered his gun and placed it on the tray next to Gracie's bed.

Danny lifted the IV stand from the floor.

Robertson said, "Step away from the gun, turn around, and put your hands on your head."

The fake doctor did as Robertson instructed.

Danny bolted out of the room.

"Danny, wait!" Robertson turned his head, just a little— and just then, he knew he'd made a mistake.

The doctor's hands were down, and he was in close.

Before Robertson had a chance to do anything, he felt something cold enter his abdomen. He lowered his gaze to see the doctor's hand on a hunting knife, and the blade was deep inside him.

Robertson tried to push back far enough to use his gun, but his attempt was futile. He began to see spots and everything around him was spinning.

Professor Wagner pulled the knife out of the detective's abdomen and then used it to slash his throat.

The detective choked on his own blood until his eyes rolled back in his head.

The professor said, "I will see you in Valhalla," and then he sprinted out of the room.

Agent Moreau was on her way back from the restroom when she spotted Danny going through a door that led to a staircase.

Just as she was about to follow him, she turned to see the German speaking doctor with a knife in his hand, and blood all over his lab coat, running in the same direction Danny had gone—toward the staircase door.

Hospital staff raced into Gracie's room.

Agent Moreau whipped out her pistol and pointed it at the bloody doctor. "Stop!"

He didn't stop.

She yelled again, "Stop or I will shoot!"

He still didn't stop, so she fired.

Two shots to the chest.

The doctor's body fell and slid across the polished floor from the momentum of him running. The knife slid across the floor even farther.

CHAPTER 60

It went against their entire life's training, but Tsomo and Miss Stong didn't want Danny to die, so Miss Stong had taken the relic to a safe place and left Tsomo with her minivan, which he had driven to the hospital.

Outside the hospital, the sun was setting and the evening air was chilly.

Tsomo circled the building, trying to formulate a plan of action in his head when he found Danny sneaking outside through a side door. He yelled, "Daniel!"

When Danny saw Tsomo, he raced toward the minivan and jumped into the passenger seat. "I take back every bad thing I said about you."

Tsomo smiled.

Danny's cheerfulness quickly faded when he spotted Victoria driving a gray Chevy Cruze, coming straight toward them. "Watch out!"

Tsomo drove as fast as he threw punches. He stepped on the gas, spun the car around, and then peeled out, almost causing Victoria to lose control of her car.

She made a U-turn while grazing a truck passing the other way then she stepped on the gas and followed them as Tsomo sped through the red light.

Danny yelled, "Holy shit!"

Two cars crossing the intersection stepped on their brakes and spun out, colliding into each other as Tsomo zipped around a pickup truck going the other way.

When Danny glanced at his side mirror, he saw that Victoria was still behind them, zigzagging with ease through the mess of smoking cars.

At first, he thought it was a rock that hit the back window, but when he turned around to look and saw that the glass was now cracked and the crack emanated from a small hole, he realized it was a bullet. "She's shooting at us!"

Tsomo swerved, almost throwing Danny out the open

window. He slipped his seatbelt on and hoped the airbags worked.

The minivan was flying.

Victoria wasn't far behind.

When they made another turn, there was road construction ahead.

Danny held his arms out in front of his face like a boxer who was ready to take a beating while Tsomo slammed on the brakes and the minivan left a trail of smoking rubber on the street.

They took out a few orange cones and clipped a white plastic barricade knocking it over and spilling the water from it while workers in hardhats and orange vests scattered.

Victoria was right behind them in the Chevy Cruze, slowing to a stop.

Danny said, "I hope you have a gun."

"I don't need a gun." Tsomo threw the shifter into reverse and slammed on the gas pedal.

The pressure on Danny's abdomen almost made him piss as the minivan shot backward and then slammed into Victoria's tiny car.

Danny could see her inside the car getting thrown around while it spun and then smashed into a van parked along the curb.

"Nice move." Danny rubbed his neck. "But at least tell me to hold on first."

Tsomo kept driving backward and then spun the minivan around the corner, just missing another minivan on the adjacent street.

Danny turned and watched Victoria stumble out of her car with something in her hand. He knew it was her gun. "She's alive!" Danny lost sight of Victoria when Tsomo turned the minivan around, shifted it into drive, and then sped forward.

Tsomo had no choice but to slow down. The light ahead had just turned red and there were at least a dozen cars and trucks between them and the intersection.

Within minutes, Victoria was right behind the minivan, this time driving a box truck.

Danny could hear the truck's engine revving hard as Victoria barreled toward them. He blocked his face with his arms and put his face between his legs.

The box truck smashed into the back of the minivan. The rear window finally shattered. Danny could hear metal compressing and other things snapping and breaking.

Tsomo stopped the minivan, jumped out, and climbed on top of it.

Danny lost sight of him. He peeked out the window and saw Victoria out of the box truck with her gun pointed at them as she marched forward. She then turned and began shooting into the air. He knew she was shooting at Tsomo. Danny forced the passenger door open and crawled out of the minivan on the other side.

Once he was out on the street, he could see Tsomo on top of the minivan. Victoria was on the other side of the truck. Danny couldn't see her, but he could hear her shooting.

Then, Danny's heart almost exploded when Tsomo fell off the minivan and landed on the street right in front of him. He raced to him, and with all of his strength, he dragged Tsomo to safety, next to the tire.

Tsomo was bleeding from the midsection, yet he seemed coherent.

Danny thought they were going to die, but just then, a cop car with his sirens on sped to the scene.

The traffic light had already turned green and the cars in front of them were gone.

The cars that came up from behind stopped before getting there.

The cop jumped out of his car and yelled at Victoria, "Drop the gun now!"

Danny heard a gunshot. He knew it was from Victoria. He wasn't going to trust just one cop to save them from her, so he helped Tsomo climb into the passenger seat of the box truck and then he climbed up and over him and closed the passenger side door before ducking down behind the steering wheel. The engine was still running.

He could now see what was going on. The cop was using his patrol car as cover while Victoria hid behind a car that had been coming the opposite way, but was now parked in the middle of the street with its doors open and no one inside. Other cars were stopped behind her, frantically trying to back up and get away from there.

Victoria fired her gun at the cop repeatedly while racing across the street to take cover behind the smashed minivan. The cop was hit. He fell backward.

Inside the box truck, Danny eyed the shifter. He had only spent three and a half weeks in truck driving school, and most of that time was in the classroom, but it was enough. He stepped on the clutch pedal, shifted into reverse, and backed up. The truck beeped in reverse.

Victoria peeked out from behind the wrecked minivan and pointed her gun at Danny.

With fear and adrenaline as his fuel, Danny kept backing up. He was ready to spin the truck around and flee, but he knew there was only one way to stop Victoria from coming after him and his family again. He had to kill her.

Victoria came out into the open and put her left hand under her right wrist to steady her shot.

Danny stepped on the clutch and slammed the shifter into first gear while stepping down on the gas pedal. The truck moved forward. He closed his eyes and ducked down.

Victoria fired. The bullet hit the windshield. It almost shattered.

Danny lifted his head just enough to see which way he had to spin the wheel.

Victoria fired before he could duck again, but luckily, her bullet took out his side mirror and not him.

In a desperate move, Danny stepped on the clutch, grinding the shit out of the gears, and then he slammed the stick shift into second. He ducked down just before the next bullet shattered the windshield.

Glass rained down onto his neck and back.

He was jolted backward as the truck slammed into the minivan.

He was afraid to look. The next of Victoria's bullets might land right between his eyes, so he ground the gears once more and then forced the truck into reverse.

Once there was enough space, he shifted into first gear and rolled forward, swerving around the smashed minivan and raising his head to peek out the passenger side window. Victoria's corpse was on the street. Mangled and covered in blood.

Danny glanced down at Tsomo slumped next to him in the passenger seat. He was unconscious but breathing.

CHAPTER 61

When Tsomo opened his eyes, he realized that it was night and that he was in the cab of a truck.

Danny was sitting next to him driving.

Tsomo felt the pain in his abdomen and tried to straighten up. "Take me to my cousin."

"I'm taking you to a hospital."

"No hospital. Take me to my cousin."

"She was my favorite teacher growing up . . . but she's not a doctor. You need to go to the hospital."

"That cannot happen. You must trust me. My injury is not serious and I am more than qualified to repair myself."

"I knew it . . . you're an android."

"A what?"

"A robot man."

Tsomo was starting to appreciate Danny's sense of humor. He laughed, but it hurt.

Danny said, "If you die . . . it's on you. I wanted to bring you to the hospital. Remember that, in case you really do come back in another life. Where does she live?"

"In your grandfather's area."

"That's far from here."

"So, it would be wise not to waste time." Tsomo felt he owed Danny the whole truth. He was a little worried that he might repeat it, but then he figured no one would ever believe him anyway. Sometimes the truth is the best lie. "You saved my life, young Daniel. And you have proven yourself an honorable man. I will tell you everything . . . but you must keep this secret even onto death. Like my cousin said, the relic is a key, but it is much more than that. It is the interface between Krishna and his Vimana." Tsomo coughed.

Danny finished making a U-turn and then turned to see Tsomo bleeding even worse than before. He drove over the speed limit while passing other cars on the street, hoping there were no cops around.

Once they were on the freeway, he was able to open it up. The evening rush hour had slowed down and traffic was now moving at a swift pace. Danny picked up speed and stayed in front of the pack along with a couple of other cars, but he was careful not to be the fastest one.

Tsomo said, "The elders always spoke of removing the key from the Vimana, but those were not Krishna's instructions, so they never did it. Now it is obvious that would have been a good idea. But then again, my people would have had to protect two different locations." Tsomo coughed, then cleared his throat and said, "There was a war . . . a war even greater than the wars we have known in the past century."

Danny listened while Tsomo told the story:

It happened thousands of years ago.

After losing an embarrassing fight against the warriors of the Yadu dynasty, the demon Salva swore his revenge against them and their lord, Krishna.

Salva ordered his most accomplished engineer to build him a new flying machine, a Vimana that could not be destroyed. The engineer built him a silver and black disk with powerful weapons and the ability to travel through air and water and he called it the Saubha. The Saubha was controlled by Salva's thoughts and it could appear as one large craft or as many smaller ones.

Hovering in his new Vimana over the ocean city of Dvaraka, Salva used bolts of lightning to destroy their buildings, streets, and gardens. His ground troops were defeated by the Yadu warriors, but their attempts to destroy the Saubha with their missiles were all in vain.

When the blue-skinned god, Krishna, returned to the region, he learned of the siege, and in his own Vimana, a fiery golden disk, he flew to the ocean city and learned that Salva had kidnapped his father.

Salva landed his Vimana on the beach and then stepped outside dragging Krishna's injured father. Salva was tall and lean with the face of a beast and he wore black silk from head to toe.

Krishna landed and stepped out of his Vimana, demanding Salva release his father. Instead, Salva taunted him, and then with a single stroke of his curved sword, Salva chopped off the old god's head.

Full of rage, Krishna charged at Salva.

Salva jumped back into his Vimana with the severed head of Krishna's father and instantly blasted into the sky, leaving only a headless corpse for Krishna to cry over.

Krishna returned to his own Vimana and gave chase.

Salva released a powerful missile that roared throughout the sky and illuminated the dark night so much that it seemed like day.

Krishna released his own barrage of smaller heat-seeking missiles that shredded Salva's great missile into a thousand pieces.

Krishna pursued Salva.

Salva's Vimana became invisible.

Krishna fired off a powerful missile that killed by seeking out sound.

Salva's new Vimana was sheared in half by Krishna's fiery weapon, but Salva was able to eject and parachute into the ocean before what was left of the Saubha erupted into flames.

Krishna landed on the beach and waited for Salva to swim to shore so he could chop off his head, just as he had done to his father. Krishna decapitated Salva and the battle ended.

The gods and the demigods rejoiced in their victory over the demons.

But the war between the gods and the demons wasn't over yet. Fierce battles in the sky and on land raged on until finally, five cities between India and Egypt, including the launching pad at Mount Sinai, were nuked, and the space station in orbit had also been destroyed.

When Krishna returned to his Tibetan mountaintop base in his damaged and smoking Vimana, his trusted human servants tended to his wounds.

Krishna's Vimana was beyond repair, so with the help of his human servants, he buried it deep in a mountain cave. They couldn't destroy it due to its nuclear power source.

Over the next few hundred years, Krishna lived high in the Tibetan mountains with his trusted servants, who he then named, The Guardians of the Secret of the Mountain.

Thousands of years passed and the gods interbred with humans until they were ultimately forgotten.

Danny's thoughts returned to the present when he noticed the freeway exit he was supposed to take . . . almost too late. He let his speed drop and then he quickly moved into the right lane and stepped on the brakes to slow down even more, but still taking the exit ramp faster than he had wanted to.

As he rolled through the stop sign and then made a turn merging into traffic on a wide street, he wondered if Tsomo was telling the truth. The relic was obviously more advanced than anything on Earth that he knew of, but he still wasn't sure if he believed everything Tsomo had just told him. Maybe it was a story meant to mislead him, or maybe he had lost so much blood that he had become delusional. But for some reason, he believed it.

Danny followed the familiar streets toward his grandfather's house.

Tsomo said, "Make the first left after your grandfather's house and then go three blocks down and make another left."

His heart felt heavy when he glanced over at his grandfather's now empty house while passing it. They knew he was ready to die, but that didn't make it any easier. Danny already missed the old man. He'd been a positive part of his life since the first day.

When he made the first left into the familiar neighborhood he asked, "Has she always lived this close?"

"The house she grew up in was about ten blocks from here. After her mother died, she moved closer to your grandfather. She never stopped believing in the mind and in our duty to retrieve it and to protect the secret of the mountain."

Danny made the next left and then slowed down.

Tsomo said, "That yellow and white house across the street."

"I still say you should be in a hospital." Danny parked the box truck in front of the yellow house and then he tried to help Tsomo up.

"Go get my cousin first."

Danny was worried Tsomo would die right there, so he raced to the front door of the house. A spotlight came on and shined right in his face. With one hand blocking the light from his eyes, Danny used his other hand to knock on the door. No answer. He knocked harder. Still no answer.

He turned to signal Tsomo that no one was answering, but because of the light in his face, Danny couldn't see into the truck. He turned back to the door and pounded on it with the bottom of his fist.

Still no answer, not even a light or a noise inside. Before turning back to go to the truck, Danny decided to try the doorknob. It was unlocked. So he turned it.

When he pushed the door open, his heart was racing. He hoped no one was in there waiting to kill him. He thought about going back to the truck and driving away, then he considered how far they were from the hospital and he worried that Tsomo might not make it that long.

He stepped into the house just far enough to hit the light switch on the wall.

The house was empty. Faded carpets and blank walls were all that was left.

Danny hurried back to the truck and opened the door.

Tsomo was gone.

On the driver's seat was the coin with a symbol on it that Tsomo wore around his neck as well as seven heavy gold coins with no markings on them.

Danny hurried around to the opposite side of the truck, but there was no sign of Tsomo.

Just as he was about to go search for him on foot, a car came out of nowhere and sped past him on the street. It was going so fast, he barely caught a glimpse of the dark green color for the fraction of a second that it was directly under the streetlamp.

CHAPTER 62

Back at her office in the federal building, Agent Moreau filled out reports on what had happened at the hospital and why she had to resort to lethal force against Professor Wilhelm. She also had to review and submit her statements about everything that had happened up to that point.

Agent Wax was busy pulling out what hair he had left on his head while yelling at a dozen young people working at computer stations.

No one knew what happened to Tsomo. They checked all the camera footage they could access yet there was no trace of him.

Agent Wax yelled, "You people aren't going home until you find him! No dinner! No breakfast! No nothing! You can piss in bottles and shit in buckets! You will not leave those computers until you find him!"

Agent Moreau wanted to tell him to take it easy, they were only human, but at the same time, she agreed with him. With every law enforcement agency searching for Tsomo and cameras at the train stations, airports, and docks as well as thousands of locations between here and there . . . how could there be no trace of him? He wasn't a ghost.

When Agent Wax approached her desk, Moreau said, "He's still here. Hiding. Waiting. He must be."

CHAPTER 63

Various government agencies questioned Danny, and after explaining everything except what Tsomo had told him about the relic's history, Danny returned to the hospital and spent the entire night on the chair next to Gracie's bed. He slept on and off. Waking up every time he thought he heard a noise or felt someone passing the room.

By the time Danny's dad arrived, sunlight was beginning to come in through the window.

"Any changes?"

Danny shook his head.

His dad said, "Go stretch your legs. I'll sit with her for a while."

He stood and kissed Gracie's head before turning to his dad. "I won't be long."

"I'll be here." He planted himself in the chair and placed his hand on Gracie's wrist.

Danny's heart felt like a transmission slipping. His eyes filled with tears and he almost cried, instead, he turned away and left the room.

The first thing he did was go to the restroom to relieve himself. He forgot he was wearing Tsomo's necklace until he saw himself in the mirror. He thought about Tsomo and hoped he got out alive.

After leaving the restroom, he headed down the long hallway to the elevator and then took it down to the first floor. He still felt as if people were after him and wondered if that feeling would ever go away.

Outside, a light breeze reminded him that he no longer had his beard and that his neck was now exposed to the elements. But he would stay that way if Gracie would have him back. If she wakes up.

He wiped the tears from his face as two middle-aged women approached the entrance. Once they went inside, he took a couple of puffs from a vape pen he had picked up at a dispensary just a few blocks away.

Feeling relaxed, Danny went back into the hospital and then headed to the cafeteria and paid too much money for an egg sandwich that was cooked in the microwave. For dessert, he enjoyed a chocolate brownie and a pint carton of milk. Before leaving, he got a cup of coffee for his dad.

Once back in Gracie's room, Danny's dad was nodding out. Danny handed him the coffee. He was expecting his dad to make a sarcastic comment about him finally having money, instead, he said, "Thanks, son."

Even though all the rooms only had one chair, no one complained when Danny dragged another chair into Gracie's room and squeezed in next to his dad.

A couple of hours passed, and both had fallen asleep.

Danny's eyes opened when Gracie's heart monitor sped up. His heart rate increased at the same time. Was she waking up? Was she having a heart attack? He could barely get the words out when he said, "Dad . . . dad . . . wake up."

His dad opened his eyes.

Danny said, "Gracie? I'm here. I love you. Please wake up." He sobbed.

Gracie opened her eyes and looked around. She couldn't speak because of the tube in her throat.

Danny couldn't stop crying. He buried his face in her neck and let it all out.

Dad hugged both of them at the same time.

It was the first time Danny had ever witnessed his father showing affection.

A nurse came in and saw what was going on, then she left and returned with a doctor.

They stayed out in the hall while the doctor removed her breathing tube and heart monitor and then took her to another room for tests.

Danny and his dad had lunch together in the cafeteria, and then a few hours later, they were allowed to return to Gracie's room where they explained everything that had happened.

When Danny's dad entered the restroom, Gracie

whispered, "He said he's proud of you."

"Who?"

"Your dad."

"My dad? Proud of me? He would never say that."

"Not to you, maybe." Replied Gracie in a hoarse voice. "But he said it to me . . . in the car . . . after you traded the box for him."

Once again, Danny's eyes filled with tears. His dad didn't have to say it to him. It only mattered that he said it. When he noticed Gracie's eyes getting watery too, he wiped both of their tears with a tissue from the box next to her bed.

Danny pretended not to know what his dad had said when he returned from the restroom, but he couldn't get it out of his head.

That night, Gracie convinced Danny to go home and sleep in his own bed. She said the black circles under his eyes were like shopping bags. He agreed, not because he was looking forward to sleeping at home, where he knew he'd be jumping out of his skin at every little sound, but because he wanted to see how much those gold coins were worth.

Danny already had the money to get his car out of impound, he just hadn't had the time. Fortunately, his father's car that had been parked in the garage was in tip-top condition, so Danny was using that.

After leaving the hospital, he dropped his dad off and then headed back to his neighborhood.

Sitting next to Gracie all that time had given him plenty of time to check his phone for places that bought gold. Danny drove to the closest one and showed the frail man behind the counter the seven gold coins. They weighed sixty grams each. The man offered Danny fifteen thousand dollars. He took it without hesitation.

On the drive home, he wondered if he could have gotten more money, but he was quickly distracted when he thought about all the things he could buy with the money he did get. He could finally replace his seven-year-old computer and get the new Pro-PlayStation. So many games and so much good weed.

For a moment, Danny thought about how jealous Skywolf was going to be . . . but then reality set in and reminded him that Skywolf was dead . . . and so was Grandpa. All of the people who had been killed over the past couple of days seemed to enter his thoughts.

Once he returned to his filthy mobile home, he decided he would clean it up, but not today. The only thing he did before going to bed was give food and water to his cats, who didn't even seem to miss him.

That night, he dreamt of murder and betrayal, which was normal by that time, and when he woke up the next morning, he thought about Detective Robertson.

On his phone, Danny located and then saved the information for Robertson's funeral, then he put on his only black suit and prepared for another funeral. His grandfather's.

Since most of Grandpa's friends and family were dead, there was a modest memorial service at the church, then Grandpa's body was cremated.

After the ceremony, Danny returned to the hospital.

Gracie beamed when she saw him in his suit. "So handsome in a suit . . . especially without all that hair on your face. If I didn't have a broken leg and a broken arm, I'd jump your bones right now."

Danny chuckled and then kissed her. "I'm gonna go home and get out of this suit. I don't want to wrinkle it . . . I'm going to wear it again tomorrow."

"Tomorrow?"

"Detective Robertson's funeral."

The next morning, it drizzled for a short time, then a dark cloudy sky and a cool wind lingered.

Danny put on his black suit and headed outside, hoping no one could tell he'd worn it the day before.

On the way there in his dad's car, he took a couple of puffs from his vape pen while listening to his favorite classic rock station on the radio.

He arrived late at the cemetery, but not too late, the reverend was in the middle of saying prayers while a huge crowd with black umbrellas tried to squeeze in closer to the coffin. There were at least a hundred cops in uniform from police departments all over Orange County and many more people in civilian clothes.

Too far away to hear anything, Danny stood there on the wet grass, waiting.

Finally, the prayers were finished and the coffin was lowered into the ground.

Robertson's widow was dressed in all black and she was trying to keep her two little boys from getting restless. She was surrounded by what appeared to be her parents and siblings as well as the mayor, the police chief, and a few other high-ranking officers.

Another half hour or so passed before the crowd had dispersed enough for Danny to approach the widow and hand her an envelope. "I'm sorry for your loss."

Her eyes and nose were red from crying and her makeup was a mess. She didn't say anything. She just lowered her head while reaching out to take it. Danny could tell by her face that she was surprised at the thickness of the envelope.

He hoped the fifteen thousand dollars would help.

If you enjoyed this book, please leave a review at:
amazon.com/author/romanbernard

Email: romanbernardauthor@gmail.com

Also from Five Borough Publishing:
Phil Nova
Author of fast-paced, suspenseful, crime thrillers for
adults.
amazon.com/author/philnova